Constance Fenimore Woolson

For the Major

A Novelette

Constance Fenimore Woolson

For the Major
A Novelette

ISBN/EAN: 9783337000776

Printed in Europe, USA, Canada, Australia, Japan

Cover: Foto ©Andreas Hilbeck / pixelio.de

More available books at **www.hansebooks.com**

"SARA HAD PREFERRED TO WALK."—[Page 71.]

𝔄 Novelette

BY

CONSTANCE FENIMORE WOOLSON

AUTHOR OF "ANNE"

ILLUSTRATED

NEW YORK

HARPER & BROTHERS, FRANKLIN SQUARE

1883

ILLUSTRATIONS.

FOR THE MAJOR.

CHAPTER I.

EDGERLEY the first lay on the eastern flank of Chillawassee Mountain; Edgerley the second six hundred feet above. The first Edgerley, being nearer the high civilization of the state capital, claimed the name, and held it; while the second Edgerley was obliged to content itself with an added "far." Far Edgerley did not object to its adjective so long as it was not considered as applying especially to the distance between it and the lower town. It was "far," if you pleased—far from cities, far from traffic, from Babylon, from Zanzibar, from the Pole—but it was not "far" from Edgerley. Rather was Edgerley far from it, and—long may she keep so! Meanwhile Edgerley the first prospered, though rather plebeianly. She had two thousand inhabitants, cheese factories, saw-mills, and a stage line across Black Mountain to Tuloa, where connection was made with a second

line, which went eastward to the railway. An Edgerley merchant, therefore, could reach the capital
of his state in fifty-five hours: what could man want
more? The merchants were of the opinion that they
wanted nothing; they fully appreciated their advantages, and Edgerley. But their neighbors on top of
the mountain, who looked down upon them in more
senses than one, did not agree with them in their
opinion; they infinitely preferred their own village,
though it had no factories, no saw-mills, no stage line
to Tuloa, and no necessity for one, and no two thousand inhabitants—hardly, indeed, and with stretching, a bare thousand. There would seem to have
been little in these lacks upon which to found a
pride, if the matter had been viewed with the eyes
of that spirit of progress which generally takes
charge of American towns; but, so far at least, the
Spirit of Progress had not climbed Chillawassee
Mountain, and thus Far Edgerley was left to its
prejudiced creed.

The creed was ancient—both towns boasting an
ante-Revolutionary origin—but, though ancient, Madam Carroll of the Farms had been the first to em-
body it in a portable phrase; brief (for more words
would have given too much importance to the subject), calmly superior, as a Carroll phrase should be.
Madam Carroll had remarked that Edgerley seemed

to her "commercial." This was excellent. "Commercial!" Nothing could be better. Whatever Far Edgerley was, it certainly was not that.

Madam Carroll of the Farms, upon a certain evening in May, 1868, was sitting in her doorway, her eyes fixed upon the dull red line of a road winding down the mountain opposite. This road was red because it ran through red clay; and a hopelessly sticky road it was, too, at most seasons of the year, as the horses of the Tuloa stage line knew to their cost. But the vehicle now coming through the last fringes of the firs was not a stage; and it was drawn, also, by two stout mules that possessed a tenacity of purpose greater even than that of red clay. It was the carriage of Major Carroll of the Farms, Far Edgerley, and at the present moment it was bringing home his daughter from the western terminus of the railway.

A gentleman's carriage drawn by mules might have seemed something of an anomaly in certain localities farther eastward. But not here. Even Edgerley regarded this possession of its rival with a respect which included the mules, or rather, which effaced them in the general aroma of the whole, an aroma not actual (the actual being that of ancient leather not unacquainted with decay), but figurative —the aroma of an undoubted aristocracy. For "the equipage," as it was called, had belonged to the Carrolls of the Sea Islands, who, in former days of opulence, had been in the habit of spending their summers at the Farms. When their distant cousin, the Major, bought the Farms, he bought the carriage also. This was as well. The Sea Island Carrolls had no longer any use for a carriage. They had not even mules to draw it, and, as they lived all the year round now upon one of their Sea Islands, whose only road through the waste of old cotton-fields was most of the time overflowed, they had nothing to draw it upon; so the Major could as well have the benefit of it. This carriage with its mules now came into sight on the zigzags of the mountain opposite; but it had still to cross the lower valley, and climb Chillawassee, and night had fallen before the sound of its wheels was heard on the little bridge over the brook which crossed what was called Carroll Lane, the grassy avenue which led from Edgerley Street up the long knoll to Carroll Farms.

"Chew up, Peter! chew up, then. Chew!" Inches, the coachman, said to his mules: Inches wished to approach the house in good style. The mules, refusing to entertain this idea, came up to the door on a slow walk. Inches could, however, let down the steps with a flourish; and this he proceeded to do by the light of the candle which Madam Carroll had brought with her to the piazza. The steps came down with a long clatter. And they had clanked in their imprisonment all the way from Tuloa. But no one in Far Edgerley would have sacrificed them for such trifles as these; they were considered to impart an especial dignity to "the equipage" (which was, indeed, rather high-hung). No other carriage west of the capital had steps of this kind. It might have been added that no other carriage east of it had them either. But Chillawassee did not know this, and went on contentedly admiring. As to the clatter made when the steps were let down — at the church door, for instance, on Sunday mornings—did it not announce that the Major and his wife had arrived, that they were about to enter? And were not people naturally glad to know this in time? They could be all ready, then, to look.

Upon this occasion the tall girl who had arrived, scarcely touching the unfolded steps, sprang lightly to the ground, and clasped the waiting lady in her arms. "Oh, mamma, how glad I am to see you again! But where is my father?"

"He felt very tired, Sara, and as it is late, he has gone to his room. He left his love for you. You know we expected you two hours ago."

"It is but little past ten. He must be still awake. Could I not slip in for a moment, just to speak to him? I would not stay."

"He has been asleep for some time. It would be better not to disturb him, wouldn't it?"

"If he is asleep—of course," answered Sara Carroll. But her tone was a disappointed one.

"You will see him in the morning," said the elder lady, leading the way within.

"But a whole night to wait is so long!"

"You do not intend, I presume, to pass this one in wakefulness?" said Madam Carroll.

Sara laughed. "Scar, too, is asleep, I suppose?"

"Yes. But Scar you can waken, if you like; he falls asleep again readily. He is in the first room at the head of the stairs."

The girl flew off, coming back with a bright face. "Dear little fellow!" she said, "his hands and cheeks are as soft as ever. I am so glad that he has not grown into a great, rough boy. It is a year and a half since I have seen him, and he seems exactly the same."

"He is the same," said Madam Carroll. "He does not grow."

"I am delighted to hear it," replied Sara, answering stoutly the mother's implied regret. And then they both laughed.

Judith Inches, sister of the coachman, now served a light repast for the traveller in the dining-room. But when it was over, the two ladies came back to the door-way.

"For I want to look out," Sara said. "I want to be sure that I am really at home at last; that this is Chillawassee, that the Black Range is opposite, and that there in the west the long line of Lonely Mountain is rising against the sky."

"As it is dark, perhaps you could see them as well from a comfortable chair in the library," suggested Madam Carroll, smiling.

"By no means. They will reveal themselves to me; you will see. I know just where they all ought to be; I made a map from the descriptions in your letters."

She had seated herself on the door-step, while Madam Carroll sat in a low chair within. Outside was a broad piazza; beyond it an old-fashioned flower-garden going down the slope of the knoll. All the earlier summer flowers were out, their presence made known in the warm, deep darkness by perfume only, save for a faint glimmer of white where the snow-ball bushes stood.

"And so, as I told you, I have decided to give an especial reception," said Madam Carroll, returning to a subject begun in the dining-room. "I shall have it on Monday; from five to eight."

"I am sorry you took the trouble, mamma. It is pleasure enough for me simply to be at home again."

"My receptions are seldom for pleasure, I think,"

said Madam Carroll, thoughtfully. "In this case it seemed proper to announce the fact that you had returned to us; that Miss Carroll would be henceforth a member of her father's household at the Farms."

"Happy girl!" interpolated Sara. She was leaning back in the door-way, her hands clasped behind her head, her eyes looking into the soft darkness of the garden.

"This was, in my opinion, a not unimportant event," continued Madam Carroll. "And it will be so estimated in Far Edgerley. There are, you know, in every society certain little distinctions and —and differences, which should be properly marked; the home-coming of Miss Carroll is one of them. You have, without doubt, an appropriate dress?"

"All my gowns are black, of course. There is one I call best; but even that is severely plain."

"On the whole, you will look well in it," answered Madam Carroll, after a moment's consideration of the figure in the door-way; "and it will have the added advantage of being a contrast. We have few contrasts in Far Edgerley, and, I may say, no plainness—no plainness whatever. Rather, a superabundance of trimming. The motive is good: I should be the last to underrate it. But even with the best intentions you cannot always construct new costumes from changes of trimming merely; there comes a

"'HAPPY GIRL,' INTERPOLATED SARA."

time when the finest skill will not take the place of a little fresh material, no matter how plain it may be. The Greers, for instance, have made over their green poplins twice a year now for five years, and have done it well. But, after all, we remain conscious that they are still the same green poplins. Miss Corinna Rendlesham, too, and her sisters, have accomplished wonders with different combinations of narrow black velvet ribbon and fringe on their black silks—so much so, indeed, that the material is now quite riddled with the old lines of needle-holes where trimmings formerly ran. They wear them to church with Stella shawls," pursued the lady, meditatively; "and to receptions, turned in at the neck, with white lace."

"Do the other people here give receptions also?" asked Sara, from the door-step.

"They would never dream of it," replied the elder lady, with serenity.

But was she the elder? No sign of age was visible in all her little person from head to foot. She was very small and slight. Her muslin gown, whose simple gathered waist was belted by a ribbon sash, had a youthful, almost childlike, aspect, yet at the same time a pretty quaintness of its own, like that of an old-fashioned miniature. The effect of this young-old attire was increased by the arrangement

2

of the hair. It was golden hair, even and fine, and it hung in curls all round her head—long curls that fell below the waist. These curls were distinct and complete spirals, each one perfect in itself, not intertwining with the next; a round stick passed through any one of them would not have been visible from bottom to top. "Now *that* is what *I* call a curl!" old Senator Ashley was wont to remark. But though this golden hair curled so definitively when it once began to curl, it lay smooth and straight as the hair of a nun over the top of the little head, and came down evenly also over the corners of the forehead, after that demure old fashion which made of every lady's brow a modest triangle, unambitious alike of a too intellectual height or a too pagan lowness.

What was it that this little *grande dame*, with her curls, her dress, and her attitudes, resembled? Some persons upon seeing her would have been haunted by a half-forgotten memory, and would at last (if clever) have recalled the pictures in the old "Annuals" and "Keepsakes" of fair ladies of the days of the Hon. Mrs. Norton and L. E. L. The little mistress of Carroll Farms needed but a scarf and harp, or a gold chain round her curls, with an ornament reposing classically in the centre of her forehead, to have taken her place among them. But upon a closer inspection one difference would have made itself apparent, namely, that whereas the lovely ladies of the "Annuals" were depicted with shoulders copiously bare (though much cloth had been expended in sleeves), the muslin gown of little Madam Carroll came up to her chin, the narrow ruffles at the top being kept in place by a child's old-fashioned necklace of coral, which fitted closely over them.

Madam Carroll's eyes were blue, large, and in expression tranquil; her features were small and delicate, the slender little lips like rose leaves, the upper one rather long, coming straight down over childlike teeth of pearl. No; certainly there was no sign of age. Yet it might have been noticed, also, by an acute observer, how little space, where such signs would have been likely to appear, was left uncovered: the tell-tale temples and outside corners of the eyes, the throat, with its faint, betraying hue, the subtly traitorous back of the neck, the texture of the wrists and palms, all these were concealed by the veil of curls and the close ruffles of the dress, the latter falling over the hands almost to the knuckles. There was really nothing of the actual woman to be seen save a narrow, curl-shaded portion of forehead and cheek, two eyes, a little nose and mouth, and the small fingers; that was all.

But a presence is more than an absence. Absent

as were all signs of age in Madam Carroll, as present
were all signs of youth in the daughter who had just
arrived. Sara Carroll was barely twenty. She was
tall and slender; she carried herself well—well, but
with a little air of pride. This air came from the
poise of her head: it was as noticeable when one
saw her back only as when one saw her face. It
seemed a pride personal, not objective, belonging to
herself, not to her surroundings; one could imagine
her with just the same air on a throne, or walking
with a basket on her arm across a prairie. But
while it was evident that she was proud, it would
have been difficult to have stated correctly the nature of the feeling, since it was equally evident that
she cherished none of the simple little beliefs often
seen in girls of her age before contact with the
world has roughly dispelled them—beliefs that they
are especially attractive, beautiful, interesting, winning, and have only to go forth to conquer. But
she herself could have stated the nature of it con-
fidently enough: she believed that her tastes, her
wishes, her ideas, possessed rather a superior quality
of refinement; but far beyond this did her pride
base itself upon the fact that she was her father's
daughter. She had been proud of this from her
birth. Her features were rather irregular, delicate.
Ordinarily she had not much color. Her straight,

soft thick hair of dark brown was put plainly back from her oval face, and this face was marked by the slender line of eyebrows of the same dusky hue, and lighted by two gray eyes, which were always, in their fair, clear color, a sort of surprise when the long, dark lashes were lifted.

"I wonder that you take the trouble," she said, referring to the proposed reception.

The blue orbs of Madam Carroll dwelt upon her for a moment. "We must fill our position," she answered. "We did not make it; it has been allotted to us. Its duties are therefore our duties."

"But are they real duties, mamma? May they not be fictitious ones? If we should drop them for a while—as an experiment?"

"If we should drop them," answered Madam Carroll—"if we should drop them, Far Edgerley, socially speaking, would disappear. It would become a miscellaneous hamlet upon a mountain-top, like any other. It would dissolve into its component parts, which are, as you know, but ciphers; we, of the Farms, hold them together, and give them whatever importance they possess."

"In other words, we, of the Farms, are the large figure One, which, placed before these poor ciphers, immediately turns them into wealth," said Sara, laughing.

"Precisely. The receptions are part of it. In addition, the Major likes them."

Sara's eyes left the soft darkness of the garden, and rested upon the speaker. "If my father likes them, that is enough. But I thought he did not; he used to speak of them, when we met at Baltimore, as so wearisome."

"Wearisome, perhaps; but still duties. And of late—that is, since you last saw him a year and a half ago—he has come to make of them a sort of pastime."

"That is so like my father! He always looks above everything narrow and petty. He can find even in poor little Far Edgerley something of interest. How glad I am to be at home again, mamma, where I can be with him all the time! I have never met any one in the world who could approach my father." She spoke warmly; her gray eyes were full of loving pride.

"He appreciates your affection. Never doubt it, in spite of what may seem to you an—an increase of reticence," said Madam Carroll.

"Father was never talkative."

"True. But he is more easily fatigued now than formerly—since his illness of last winter, you know. But it is growing late; I must close the house."

"Do you do that yourself?"

"Generally. I seldom keep Judith Inches up after half-past nine. And on ordinary occasions I am in bed myself soon after ten. Your home-coming is an extraordinary one."

"And extraordinarily glad it makes me," said Sara. "I wonder, mamma, if you know how glad? I have fairly pined during this last year and a half at Longfields—yes, in spite of all Uncle John's kindness. Do you think me heartless?"

"No," said Madam Carroll, as they went up the stairs together. "You loved your uncle, I know. You did your best to make him happy. But your father, Sara—your father, you have always adored."

"And I continue to do it," answered the daughter, gayly. "I shall be down early, early in the morning to see him."

"He does not come to breakfast at present. His strength has not yet fully returned. I have written you of this."

"Not that he did not come to breakfast, mamma. That is so unlike him; he was always so cheerful and bright at the breakfast-table. But at least I can take his breakfast in to him?"

"I think he would rather see you later—about ten, or half-past."

A flush rose in Sara's face: no one would have called her colorless now. She looked hurt and an-

gry. "Pray, who does take in his breakfast, then?"
she asked. "I should think I might be as welcome
as Judith Inches."

"I take it," replied Madam Carroll, gently.

"Very well, mamma; I will not begin by being
jealous of you?"

"You never have been, my daughter. And I—
have appreciated it." Madam Carroll spoke in low
tones: they were approaching the Major's door. She
pointed towards it warningly. "We must not waken
him," she said. She led her daughter in silence to
the room she had fitted up for her with much taste
and care. They kissed each other, and separated.

Left alone, Sara Carroll looked round her room.
As much had been done to make it bright as woman's hands, with but a small purse to draw upon,
could accomplish. The toilet-table, the curtains, the
low lounge, with its great, cool, chintz-covered pillows, the hanging shelves, the easy-chair, the writing-
table—all these were miracles of prettiness and in-
genuity. But the person for whom this had been
done saw it but vaguely. She was thinking of only
one thing—her father; that he had not waited to
welcome her; that she should not see him until
half-past ten the next morning. What could this
mean? If he were ill, should not his daughter be
the first to see him, the first to take care of him?

She had told Madam Carroll that she would not begin the new home life by being jealous of her. But there was something very like jealousy in the disappointment which filled her heart as she laid her head upon the pillow. She had looked forward to her home-coming so long; and now that she held it in her grasp it was not at all what she had been sure it would be.

Upon this same Saturday evening, at dusk, light was shining from the porch and windows of St. John in the Wilderness, the Episcopal church of Far Edgerley. This light shone brightest from the porch, for there was a choir rehearsal within, and the four illuminating candles were down by the door, where stood the organ. Two of the candles illumined the organist, Miss Rendlesham the second, that is, Miss Millie; the others lighted the high music-stand, behind which stood the choir in two rows, the first very crowded, the second looking with some difficulty over the shoulders of the first at the light-ed books which served for both, little Miss Tappen, indeed, who was short, being obliged to stand on four unused chant-books, piled. In the front row were the soprani, eight in number, namely, Miss Rendlesham the elder, and her sister; the three Misses Greer; Miss Dalley and her two cousins, the Farrens, who were (which was so interesting) twins.

In the back row were the two contralti, Miss Bolt
and the already-mentioned Miss Tappen on her
books, together with the tenor, Mr. Phipps; there,
too, was the basso, Mr. Ferdinand Kenneway, a bach-
elor of amiable aspect, but the possessor also, in spite
of amiability, of several singularly elusive qualities
which had tried the patience of not a few.

The music-stand, no doubt, was very much too
short for this company. But then it was intended
for a quartette only, and had served without question for four estimable persons during the long,
peaceful rectorship of good old Parson Montgomery, who had but recently passed away. Since the
advent of his successor, the Reverend Frederick
Owen, three months before, the choir had trebled
its size without trebling that of the stand; the result was naturally that which has been described.

The Reverend Frederick Owen was an unmarried
man.

St. John in the Wilderness had as its rector's
study a little one-story building standing in the
church-yard, not far from the church; on Saturday
evenings the rector was generally there. Upon the
present evening Miss Rendlesham the elder, that is,
Miss Corinna, sent the juvenile organ-blower, Alexander Mann by name, across to this study for the
numbers of the hymns, as usual. But the rector did

not return with Alexander Mann, as usual, bringing the hymns with him: he sent the numbers, written on a slip of paper. Under these circumstances the choir began its practising. And its practising was, on the whole, rather spiritless. That is, in sound, but not in continuance; for, two hours later, they were still bravely at work. The time had been principally filled with *Te Deums*. During the past three months the choir had had a new *Te Deum* every Sunday—to the discomfiture of Senator Ashley, who liked to join in "old Jackson's."

This gentleman, who was junior warden, had dropped in, soon after Alexander Mann's departure with the hymns, to talk over some church matters with the rector. The church matters finished, he remained a while longer to talk over matters more secular. The junior warden had a talent for talking. But this gift (as is often the case with gifts) was not encouraged at home, Miss Honoria Ashley, his daughter, not being of a listening disposition. The junior warden was therefore obliged to carry his talent elsewhere. He was a small old gentleman, lean and wizened, but active, and even lively, in spite of his age, save for a harassing little cough, which could, however, end with surprising adaptation to circumstances in either a chuckle or a groan. The possessor of this cough wore an old-fashioned dress-coat, with a high stock and very neat, shining little shoes. He had always in his button-hole a flower in summer, and in winter a geranium leaf.

The chanting of the choir came through the open windows. "I should think they would be exhausted over there," he said. "How long do they keep it up? Ferdinand Kenneway must be voiceless by this time. He has only a thread of a voice to begin with."

"He sings with unusual correctness, I believe," said the rector.

"Oh, he's *correct*—very! It's his only characteristic. I don't know of any other, unless you include his health: he lives principally for the purpose of not taking cold. Your choir is rather predominately feminine just now, isn't it?" added the old gentleman, slyly.

"Choirs are apt to be, are they not? I mean the volunteer ones. For the women everywhere come to church far more than the men do. It is one of the problems with which clergymen of the present day find tl.emselves confronted."

"That the women come?"

"That the men do not." The rector spoke gravely. He was but little over thirty himself, yet he had been obliged more than once to put a mildly restraining pressure upon the somewhat too active gay-mindedness of his venerable junior warden.

" What's that thing they're trying now ?" said this official, abandoning his jocularity. " Dull and see-saw it sounds to me ; dull and see-saw."

" It's a *Te Deum* I selected for Trinity Sunday."

" Ah, if *you* selected it— But it can never equal ' old Jackson's,' never ! That's Sophy Greer on the solo. She can no more do it than a consumptive hen. But, sir, I'll tell you who can—Sara Carroll. They expect her home to-night."

" Madam Carroll's daughter ?"

" No, the Major's. Madam Carroll is the Major's second wife—didn't you know that ? Sara Carroll, sir, can never hope to equal her step - mother in beauty, grace, or charm. But she is a fine girl in her way—as indeed she ought to be : her mother was a Witherspoon-Meredith."

The rector looked unimpressed. The junior war-den, seeing this, drew up his chair. " The Wither-spoon - Merediths, Mr. Owen, are one of our oldest families." (The rector resigned himself.) " When Scarborough Carroll married the beautiful Sara of that name, a noble pair they were, indeed, as they stood at the altar. I speak, sir, from knowledge : *I* was *there*. Their children—two boys—died, to their great grief. The last child was this daughter Sara ; and the accomplished mother passed away soon after the little thing's birth. Sir, Major Carroll, your sen-

ior warden, has always been one of our grandest
men ; in personal appearance, character, and distinguished services, one of the noblest sons of our state.
Of late he has not, perhaps, been *quite* what he was
physically ; but the change is, in my opinion, entirely due—entirely—to his own absurd imprudences.
For he is still in the prime of life, the very prime."
(Major Carroll was sixty - nine ; but as the junior
warden was eighty-five, he naturally considered his
colleague still quite a boy.) "Until lately, however,
he has been undeniably, I will not say one of nature's princes, because I do not believe in them, but
one of the princes of the Carrolls, which is saying a
vast deal more.   His little girl has always adored
him.   He has been, in fact, a man to inspire admiration.   To give you an idea of what I mean : a half-
brother of his, much older than himself, and broken
in health, lost, by the failure of a bank, all he had in
the world.   He was a married man, with a family.
Carroll, who was at that time a young lieutenant
just out of West Point, immediately shared his own
property with this unfortunate relative.   He didn't
dole out help, keeping a close watch over its use, or
grudgingly give so much a year, with the constant
accompaniment of good advice ; he simply deeded a
full half of all he had to his brother, and never
spoke of it again.   Forty-five years have passed, and

he has never broken this silence; the brother is dead, and I doubt if the children and grandchildren who profited by the generous act even know to whom they are indebted. Such, sir, is the man, chivalrous, unsullied, true. In 1861 he gave his sword to his state, and served with great gallantry throughout the war. He was twice severely wounded; you may have noticed that his left arm is stiff. When our Sacred Cause was lost, with the small remains of his small fortune he purchased this old place called the Farms, and here, sir, he has come, to pass the remainder of his days in, as I may well say, the Past—the only country left open to him, as indeed to many of us." And the old gentleman's cough ended in the groan.

"And Miss Carroll has not been with them here?" asked the rector, giving the helm of conversation a slight turn from this well-beaten track.

"No, she has not. But there have been good reasons for it. To give you the causes, I must make a slight detower into retrospect. At a military post in Alabama, when Sara was about seven years old, the Major met the lady who is now Madam Carroll; she was then a widow named Morris, with one child, a little girl. You have seen this lady for yourself, sir, and know what she is—a domestic angel, yet a very Muse in culture; one of the loveliest women,

one of the most engaging, upon my word, that ever
walked the face of this earth, and honored it with
her tread." (The junior warden spoke with enthusiasm.) "She is of course very much younger than
her husband, *thir*-ty three or four years at the least,
I should say; for Carroll was fifty-six at the time of
his second marriage, though no one would have suspected it. I saw Madam Carroll very soon afterwards, and she could not have been then more than
twenty one or two; a little fairy-like girl-mother.
She must have been married the first time when not
more than sixteen. Later they had a son, the boy
you know, who is now, save Sara, the only child."

"Ah, I see; I understand," said the rector.

But the junior warden did not; his understand-
ing was that there was more to tell. He drew up
his chair again. "Sara Carroll, sir, is a remarkable
girl." (The rector again resigned himself.) "She
is, as I may say, one-ideaed. By that I mean that
she has had from childhood one feeling so predomi-
nant that she has fairly seemed to have but the one,
which is her devotion to her father. She had scarcely been separated from him (save, as it happens,
during the very summer when he met and married
the present Madam Carroll) until she was a tall girl
of thirteen. This was in 1861. At that time, before the beginning of actual hostilities, her uncle,

John Chase—he had married her mother's sister— offered to take her and have her educated with his own daughter Euphemia during the continuance of the troubled times. For John Chase had always been very fond of the little Sara; he fancied that she was like his wife. And, cold New-Englander though he was, he had worshipped his wife (she was Juliet Witherspoon-Meredith), and seemed to be always thinking of her, though she had been dead many years. The Major at first refused. But Madam Carroll, with her exquisite perception, perfect judgment, and beautiful goodness" (the junior warden always spoke in at least triplets of admiration when he mentioned the Major's wife), "explained to him the benefit it would be to Sara. Her own lot was cast with his; she would not have it otherwise; but in the wandering life she expected to lead, following his fortunes through the armed South, what advantages in the way of education should she be able to secure for his little daughter, who was now of an age to need them? Whereas her uncle, who was very fond of her, would give her many. The Major at last yielded. And then Sara was told. Well as they knew her, I think they were both alarmed at the intensity of her grief. But when the poor child saw how it was distressing her father, she controlled it, or rather the expression of

3

it; and to me her self-control was more touching
even than her tears had been, for one could see that
her innocent heart was breaking. The parting was
a most pathetic sight—her white cheeks, silence, and
loving, despairing eyes, that never left her father's
face—I don't know when I have been more affected.
For I speak from personal remembrance, sir: *I* was
there. Well, that little girl did not see her father
again for four long years. She lived during that
time with her uncle at Longfields—one of those villages of New England with still, elm-shaded, conscientious streets, silent white houses, the green
blinds all closed across their broad fronts, yet the
whole pervaded too, in spite of this quietude, by an
atmosphere of general, unresting *interrogativeness*,
which is, as I may say, sir, *strangling* to the unac-
customed throat. I speak from personal remembrance; I have been *personally* there."

"I do not think there is now as much of—of the
atmosphere you mention, as there once was," said
the rector, smiling.

"Perhaps not, perhaps not. But when I was there
you breathed it in every time you opened your
mouth—like powdered alum. But to ree-vee-nir (I
presume you are familiar with the French expression). In those four years Sara Carroll grew to
womanhood; but she did not grow in her feelings;

she remained one-ideaed. Mind you, I do not, while describing it, mean in the least to commend such an affection as hers; it was unreasonable, overstrained. I should be very sorry indeed, extremely sorry, to see my daughter Honoria making such an idol of me."

The rector, who knew Miss Honoria Ashley, her aspect, voice, and the rules with which she barred off the days of the poor old junior warden, let his eyes fall upon his well-scrubbed floor (scrubbed twice a week, under the personal supervision of Mrs. Rendlesham, by the Rendlesham's maid-of-all-work, Lucilla.

"But the Ashleys are always of a calm and reasonable temperament, I am glad to say," pursued the warden, "a temperament that might be classified as judicial. Honoria is judicial. To ree-vee-nir. Sara was about seventeen when her father bought this place, called the Farms, and nothing, I suppose, could have kept her from coming home at that time but precisely that which did keep her—the serious illness of the uncle to whom she owed so much. His days were said to be numbered, and he wanted her constantly beside him. I am inclined to suspect that his own daughter, Euphemia, while no doubt a highly intellectual person, may not have a—a natural aptitude for those little tendernesses of voice, touch,

and speech—unprescribed if you like, but most dear
—which to a sick man, sir, are beyond rubies, far
beyond." The old man's eyes had a wistful look as
he said this; he had forgotten for the moment his
narrative, and even Miss Honoria; he was thinking
of Miss Honoria's mother, his loving little wife, who
had been long in paradise.

He went on with his story, but less briskly. "Sara,
therefore, has remained at Longfields with her uncle.
But every six months or so she has come down as
far as Baltimore to meet her father, who has journeyed northward for the purpose, with Madam Carroll, the expense of these meetings being gladly
borne by John Chase, whose days could not have
been so definitely numbered, after all, as he supposed,
since he has lingered on indefinitely all this time,
nearly three years. During the last year and a half,
too, he has been so feeble that Sara could not leave
him, the mere thought of an absence, however short,
seeming to prey upon him. She has not, therefore,
seen her father since their last Baltimore meeting,
eighteen months back, as the Major himself has not
been quite well enough to undertake the long journey to Connecticut. Chase at length died, two
months ago, and she has now come home to live.
From what I hear," added the warden, summing up,
"I am inclined to think that she will prove a very

fair specimen of a Witherspoon and Meredith, if not quite a complete Carroll."

"And she could sing the solo for us on Trinity Sunday?" said the rector, giving the helm a turn towards his anthem.

"She *could*," said the warden, with impartial accent, retreating a little when he found himself confronted by a date.

"Do you mean if she would?"

"Well, yes. She is rather distant—reserved; I mean, that she seems so to strangers. You won't find *her* offering to sing in your choir, or teach in your Sunday-school, or bring you flowers, or embroider your book-marks, or make sermon-covers for you, or dust the church, or have troubles in her mind which require your especial advice; *she* won't be going off to distant mission stations on Sunday afternoons, walking miles over red-clay roads, and jumping brooks, while you go comfortably on your black horse. She'll be rather a contrast in St. John's just now, won't she?" And the warden's cough ended in the chuckle.

It was now after ten, and the choir was still practising. Mr. Phipps, indeed, had proposed going home some time before. But Miss Corinna Rendlesham having remarked in a general way that she pitied "poor puny men" whose throats were always "giving out," he knew from that that she would not go herself nor allow Miss Lucy to go. Now Miss Lucy was the third Miss Rendlesham, and Mr. Phipps greatly admired her. Ferdinand Kenneway, wiser than Phipps, made no proposals of any sort (this was part of his correctness); his voice had been gone for some time, but he found the places for everybody in the music-books, as usual, and pretended to be singing, which did quite as well.

"I am convinced that there is some mistake about this second hymn," announced Miss Corinna (after a fourth rehearsal of it); "it is the same one we had only three Sundays ago."

"Four, I think," said Miss Greer, with feeling. For was not this a reflection upon the rector's memory?

"Oh, very well; if it *is* four, I will say nothing. I *was* going to send Alexander Mann over to the study to find out—supposing it to be three only—if there might not be some mistake."

At this all the other ladies looked reproachfully at Miss Greer.

She murmured, "But your fine powers of remembrance, dear Miss Corinna, are *far* better than mine."

Miss Corinna accepted this; and sent Alexander Mann on his errand. Ferdinand Kenneway, in the dusk of the back row, smiled to himself, thinly; but as nature had made him thin, especially about the cheeks, he was not able to smile in a richer way.

During the organ-boy's absence the choir rested. The voices of the ladies were, in fact, a little husky.

"No, it's all right; that's the hymn he meaned," said Alexander Mann, returning. "An' I ast him if he weern't coming over ter-night, an' he says, 'Oh yes!' says he, an' he get up. Old Senator Ashley's theer, an' *he* get up too. So I reckon the parson's comin', ladies." And Alexander smiled cheerfully on the row of bonnets as he went across to his box beside the organ.

But Miss Corinna stopped him on the way. "What could have possessed you to ask questions of your rector in that inquisitive manner, Alexander Mann?" she said, surveying him. "It was a piece of great impertinence. What are his intentions or his non-intentions to you, pray?"

"Well, Miss Corinna, it's orful late, an' I've blowed an' blowed till I'm clean blowed out. An' I knewed that as long as the parson stayed on over theer, you'd all—"

"All what?" demanded Miss Corinna, severely.

But Alexander, frightened by her tone, retreated to his box.

"Never mind him, dear Miss Corinna," said little

Miss Tappen, from behind; "he's but a poor mother-less orphan."

"Perhaps he is, and perhaps he is *not*," said Miss Corinna. "But in any case he must finish his sentence: propriety requires it. Speak up, then, Alexander Mann."

"I'll stand by you, Sandy," said Mr. Phipps, humorously.

"You said," pursued Miss Corinna, addressing the box, since Alexander was now well hidden within it —"you said that as long as the rector remained in his study, you knew—"

"I knewed you'd all hang on here," said Alexander, shrilly, driven to desperation, but safely invisible within his wooden retreat.

"Does he mean anything by this?" asked Miss Corinna, turning to the soprani.

"I am sure we have not remained a moment beyond our usual time," said Miss Greer, with dignity.

"I ask you, does he *mean* anything?" repeated Miss Corinna, sternly.

"Oh, dear Miss Corinna, I am sure he has no meaning at all — none whatever. He never has," said good-natured little Miss Tappen, from her piled chant-books. "And he weeds flower-beds *so* well!"

Here voices becoming audible outside, the ladies stopped; a moment later the rector entered. His junior warden was not with him. Having recollected suddenly the probable expression upon Miss Honoria's face at this hour, the junior warden had said good-night, paced down the knoll and up Edgerley Street with his usual careful little step until the safe seclusion of Ashley Lane was reached, when, laying aside his dignity, he took its even moonlit centre, and ran, or rather trotted, as fast as he could up its winding ascent to his own barred front door, where Miss Honoria let him in, candle in hand, and on her head the ominous cap (frilled) which was with her the expression of the hour. For Miss Honoria always arranged her hair for the night and put on this cap at ten precisely; thus crowned, and wrapped in a singularly depressing gray shawl, she was accustomed to wait for the gay junior warden, when (as had at present happened) he had forgotten her wishes and the excellent clock on her mantel that struck the hours. Meanwhile the rector was speaking to his choir about the selections for Trinity Sunday. He addressed Miss Corinna. At rehearsals he generally addressed Miss Corinna. This was partly due to her martial aspect, which made her seem the natural leader far more than Phipps or Kenneway, but principally because, being well over fifty, she was no longer troubled by the flutter of embarrassment with which the other ladies seemed

to be oppressed whenever he happened to speak to
them—timid young things as they were, all of them
under thirty-five.

Miss Corinna responded firmly. The other ladies
maintained a gently listening silence. At length
the rector, having finished all he had to say, glanced
at his watch. " Isn't it rather late?" he said.

And they were all surprised to find how late it
was.

Like a covey of birds rising, they emerged from
the pen made by the music-stand and organ, and
moved in a modest group towards the door. The
rector remained behind for a moment to speak to
Bell-ringer Flower. When he came out, they were
still fluttering about the steps and down the front
path towards the gate. " I believe our roads are
the same," he said.

As indeed they were: there was but one road
in Far Edgerley. This was called Edgerley Street,
and all the grassy lanes that led to people's resi-
dences turned off from and came back to it, going
nowhere else. There were advantages in this. Some
persons had lately felt that they had not sufficiently
appreciated this excellent plan for a town ; for if
any friend should happen to be out, paying a visit
or taking the air, sooner or later, with a little patience, one could always meet her (or him); she (or

he), without deliberate climbing of fences, not being able to escape.

The little company from the church now went down the church knoll towards this useful street. Far Edgerley was all knolls, almost every house having one of its own, and crowning it. The rector walked first, with Miss Corinna; the other ladies followed in a cluster which was graceful, but somewhat indefinite as to ranks, save where Mr. Phipps had determinedly placed himself beside Miss Lucy Rendlesham, and thus made one even rank of two. Ferdinand Kenneway walked by himself a little to the right of the band; he walked not with any one in particular, but as general escort for the whole. Ferdinand Kenneway often accompanied Far Edgerley ladies homeward in this collective way. It was considered especially safe.

Flower, the bell-ringer, left alone on the church steps, looked after their departing figures in the moonlight. "A riddler it is," he said to himself—— "a riddler, and a myst'rous one, the way all womenkind feels itself drawed to parsons. I suppose they jedge anything proper that's clirrycal." He shook his head, locked the church door, and went across to close the study.

Flower was a Chillawassee philosopher who had formerly carried the mail on horseback over Lonely

Mountain to Fox Gap. Age having dimmed somewhat his youthful fires, lessening thereby his interest in natural history, as exemplified by the bears,
wolves, and catamounts that diversified his route, he
had resigned his position, judging it to be "a little
too woodsy," on the whole, for a man of his years.
He then accepted the office of bell-ringer of St.
John's, a place which he had been heard to say conferred a dignity second only to that of mails. He
was very particular about this dignity, and the title
of it. "Item," he said, "that I be not a sexton ; for
sexton be a slavish name for a free-born mountaineer. Bell-ringer Flower I be, and Bell-ringer
Flower you may call me."

Now the bell of St. John's was but a small one,
suspended rustically, under a little roof of thatch,
from the branch of an old elm near the church
door ; to ring it, therefore, was but a slight task.
But Flower made it a weighty one by his attitude
and manner as he stood on Sunday mornings, rope
in hand, hat off, and eyes devotionally closed, beside
his leafy belfry, bringing out with majestic pull the
one little silver note.

He now re-arranged the chairs in the study, and
came upon a framed motto surrounded by rosebuds
in worsted-work, a fresh contribution to the rector's
walls from the second Miss Greer. "Talk about

the mil'try—my! they're nothing to 'em—nothing to these unmarried reverints!" he said to himself, as he surveyed this new memento. He hung it on the wall, where there was already quite a frieze of charming embroidery in the way of texts and woollen flowers. "Item—however, very few of them *is* unmarried. Undoubted they be drove to it early, in self-defence."

CHAPTER II.

"You are a little tired, Major?"

"Possibly. Somewhat. Sara has been reading aloud to me from the *Review*. She read all the long articles."

"Ah—she does not know how that tires you. I must tell her. She does not appreciate—she is still so young, you know—that with your extensive reading, your knowledge of public affairs and the world at large, you can generally anticipate, after the first few sentences, all that can be said."

The Major did not deny this statement of his resources.

"I am going to the village for an hour or two," continued Madam Carroll; "I shall take Sara with me." (Here the Major's face seemed to evince a certain relief.) "We must call upon Miss Honoria Ashley. And also at Chapultepec, upon Mrs. Hibbard."

"Yes, yes — widow of General Hibbard, of the Mexican War," said the Major, half to himself.

" I do not pay many visits, as you know, Major ; our position does not require it. We open our house — that is enough ; our friends come to us ; they do not expect us to go to them. But I make an exception in the case of Mrs. Hibbard and of Miss Ashley, as you have advised me to do ; for the Ashleys are connected with the Carrolls by marriage, though the tie is remote, and Mrs. Hibbard's mother was a Witherspoon. I know you wish Sara to understand and recognize these little distinctions and differences."

"Certainly. Very proper," said the Major.

" We shall be gone an hour and a half, perhaps two hours. I will send Scar to you for his lessons ; and I shall tell Judith Inches to allow no one to disturb you, not even to knock at this door. For Scar's lessons are important, Major."

" Yes, very important—very."

" Good-bye, then," said his wife, cheerfully, resting her hand on his shoulder for a moment, as she stood beside his chair. The Major drew the slender hand forward to his gray moustache.

" Fie, Major ! you spoil me," said the little woman, laughing.

She left the room, making, with her light dress and long curls, a pretty picture at the door, as she turned to give him over her shoulder a farewell nod

and smile. The Major kept on looking at the closed
door for several minutes after she had gone.

Not long after this the same door opened, and a
little boy came in ; his step was so light and his
movements so careful that he made no sound. He
closed the door, and laid the book he had brought
with him upon a table. He was a small, frail child,
with a serious face and large blue eyes ; his flaxen
hair, thin and fine, hung in soft, scanty waves round
his little throat—a throat which seemed too small
for his well-developed head, yet quite large enough
for his short, puny body. He was dressed in a blue
jacket, with an embroidered white collar reaching to
the shoulders, and ruffles of the same embroidery at
the knee, where his short trousers ended. A blue
ribbon tied his collar, and his slender little legs and
feet were incased in long white stockings and low
slippers, such as are worn by little girls. His whole
costume, indeed, had an air of effeminacy ; but he
was such a delicate-looking little fellow that it was
not noticeable. From a woman's point of view, he
was prettily dressed.

He crossed the room, opened a closet door, and
took from a shelf two boxes, which he carried to
the table, making a separate journey with each. He
arranged these systematically, the book in the centre, a box on each side ; then he pushed the table

over the carpet towards the Major's chair. The table was narrow and light, and made no sound. He moved onward slowly, his hands, widely apart, grasping its top, and he paused several times to peer round the corner of it so as to bring it up within an inch of the Major's feet, yet not to touch them. This accomplished, he surveyed the position gravely. Satisfied with it, he next brought up a chair for himself, which, while not the ordinary high-chair of a child, seemed yet to have been made especially for him on account of his low stature. He drew this chair close to the table on the opposite side, climbed into it, and then, when all was prepared, he spoke. "I am quite ready now, papa, if you please." His slender little voice was clear and even, like his mother's; his words followed each other with slow precision.

The Major woke, or, if he had not been asleep, opened his eyes. "Ah, little Scar," he said, "you here?" And he patted the child's hand caressingly. Scar opened his book; then one of the boxes, which contained white blocks with large red letters painted upon them. He read aloud from the book a sentence, once, twice. Then he proceeded to make it from memory with the blocks on the table, working slowly, and choosing each letter with thoughtful deliberation.

4

" Good — blood — can — not — lie," he read aloud from his row of letters when the sentence was completed. " I think that is right. Your turn, papa."

And then the Major, with almost equal slowness, formed, after Scar had read it, the following adage : " A brave father makes a brave son." " That's you and I, Scar."

" Yes, papa. And this is the next : ' The—knights —are—dust.—Their—good—swords—rust.—Their —souls—are—with—the—saints—we—trust.' That is too long for one. We will call it three."

Father and little son completed in this slow way eight of the sentences the little book contained. It was a small, flat volume in manuscript, the letters clearly printed with pen and ink. The Major's wife had prepared it, " from the Major's dictation," she said. " A collection of the fine old sayings of the world, which he greatly admires, and which he thinks should form part of the preliminary education of our son."

" Eight. The lesson is finished, papa," said Scar. " If you think I have done sufficiently well, I may now amuse myself with my dominoes." As he spoke he replaced the letters in their box, put on the cover, and laid the manuscript book on the top. Then he drew forward the second box, and took out his dominoes. He played by himself, one hand against the other. "You will remember, papa, that my right hand I call Bayard and my left Roland."

"Yes," answered the Major, looking on with interest.

Roland won the first game. Then the second. "The poor chevalier seems to have no luck to-day. I must help him a little," said the Major. And he and Scar played a third game.

While they were thus engaged, with Bayard's fortunes not much improved as yet, the door opened, and Sara Carroll came in. The Major was sitting with his spectacles on and head bent forward, in order to read the numbers on the dominoes; his hand, poised over the game while he considered his choice, had the shrivelled appearance, with the veins prominent on the back, which more than anything else betrays the first feebleness of old age. As his daughter came in he looked up, first through his spectacles, then, dropping his head a little, over them, after the peering fashion of old men. But the instant he recognized her his manner, attitude, even his whole appearance, changed, as if by magic; his spectacles were off; he had straightened himself, and risen. "Ah! you have returned?" he said. "Scar had his lessons so well that I have permitted him to amuse himself with his dominoes for a while, as you see. You are back rather sooner than you expected, aren't you?"

"We had to postpone our visit to Mrs. Hibbard,"
said Sara.

The Major's lips formed, "of the Mexican War;"
but he did not utter the syllables aloud, and immediately thereafter seemed to take himself more vigor-
ously in hand, as it were. He walked to the hearth-
rug, and took up a position there with his shoulders
back, his head erect, and one hand in the breast of
his frock-coat. "It is quite proper that you should
go to see those two ladies, my daughter; the Ashleys are connected with the Carrolls by marriage,
though the tie is a remote one, and the mother of
Mrs.—Mrs.—the other lady you were mentioning;
her name has just escaped me—"

"Hibbard," said Sara.

"Yes, Mrs. Hibbard of the Mex— I mean, that
Mrs. Hibbard's mother was a Witherspoon. It is
right that you should recognize these—ah, these little distinctions and differences." He brought out the
last words in full, round tones. The Major's voice
had always been a fine one.

He was a handsome, soldierly-looking man, tall,
broad-shouldered, with noble bearing, and bold, well-
cut features. He was dressed in black, with broad,
stiff, freshly starched white cuffs, and a high standing collar, round which was folded a black silk cravat
that when opened was three-quarters of a yard square.

His thin gray hair, moustache, and imperial were cut after the fashion affected by the senior officers of the old army—the army before the war.

"They are not especially interesting in themselves, those two ladies," remarked his daughter, taking off her little black bonnet. "Miss Honoria cares more about one's shoes—whether or not they are dusty enough to injure her oiled floors—than about one's self ; and Mrs. Hibbard talks all the time about her ducks."

"True, quite true. Those ducks are extremely tiresome. I have had to hear a great deal about them myself," said the Major, in an injured tone, forgetting for a moment his military attitude. "What do I know of ducks? Yet she *will* talk about them."

"Why should you listen ?" said Sara, drawing off her gloves.

"Ah, we must not forget that her mother was a Mex—I mean, a Witherspoon. It is not necessary for us, for you, to pay many visits, my daughter; our position does not require it. We—ah—we open our house ; that is enough ; our friends come to us; they do not expect us to go to them."

Sara was now taking off her mantle; he watched to see whether she would keep it or put it down. She threw it over her arm, and she also took up her bonnet and gloves. "You will let me come back and read to you, father?"

"Thank you, my dear; but it is not necessary. I have still another of Scar's lessons to attend to, and Scar's lessons are important, very important. There are, besides, various other little things which may require my attention. In short, my—ah—mornings are at present quite filled. Besides, reading aloud is very fatiguing, very; and I do not wish you to fatigue yourself on my account."

"Nothing I was doing for you could fatigue me, father. You don't know how I have longed to be at home again so that I *could* do something for you." She spoke warmly.

The Major looked perturbed. He coughed, and glanced helplessly towards the door. As if in answer to his look, the door at that moment opened, and his wife came in.

"Mr. Owen is in the drawing-room, Sara," she said. "Will you go in and see him, please? I will follow you in a moment. I met him on his way here, and offered him your vacant place in the carriage."

"He comes rather often, doesn't he?" said Sara, her eyes still on her father's face.

"Yes, he comes often. But it is natural that he should wish to come. As the Major has observed before this, the rector of St. John's must always rely for his most congenial society, as well as for something of guidance, too, upon Carroll Farms."

"Certainly," said the Major. "I have often made the remark."

"I suppose he comes more especially to see you, father," Sara said.

"Mr. Owen knows that he must not expect to see the Major in the morning," said Madam Carroll. "The Major's mornings are always occupied, and he prefers not to be interrupted. In fact, it is not Mr. Owen, but you and I, Sara, who have been the chief sinners in this respect of late; we must amend our ways. But come, you should not keep the rector waiting too long, or he will think that your Northern education has relaxed the perfection of your Carroll manners."

She took her daughter's arm, and they left the room together. But only a few minutes had elapsed when the little wife returned. "Go get your father's glass of milk, my pet," she said to Scar.

The boy climbed down from his place at the table, and left the room with his noiseless step. The Major was leaning back in his easy-chair, with his eyes closed; he looked tired.

"We went to the Ashleys'," said his wife, taking a seat beside him. "But there we learned that Mrs.

Hibbard was confined to her bed by an attack of rheumatism, brought on, they think, by her having remained too long in the duck-yard; and so we were obliged to postpone our visit to Chapultepec. I then decided to take the time for some necessary household purchases, and as Sara knows as yet but little of my method of purchasing, I arranged to leave her at Miss Dalley's (Miss Dalley has been so anxious to talk over Tasso with her, you know), and call for her on my return. But she must have soon tired of Miss Dalley, for she did not wait; she walked home alone."

"Yes, she came in here. She has been here a long time," answered the Major. Then he opened his eyes. "It was in the midst of Scar's lessons," he said, as if explaining.

"Ah, I see. That must not happen again. She will at once understand—that is, when I explain it—that Scar's lessons should not be interrupted. She is very fond of Scar. You will have your lunch in here to-day, won't you, Major? I think it would be better. It is Saturday, you know, and on Saturdays we all rest before the duties of Sunday—duties which, in your case especially, are so important."

But the Major seemed dejected. "I don't know about that—about their being so important," he answered. "Ashley is always there."

"Oh, Major! Major! the idea of your comparing yourself with Godfrey Ashley! He is all very well in his way—I do not deny that; but he is not and never can be *you*. Why, St. John's would not know itself, it would not be St. John's, if you were not there to carry round the plate on Sunday mornings. And everybody would say the same." She laid her hand on his forehead, not with a light, uncertain touch, but with that even pressure which is grateful to a tired head. The Major seemed soothed; he did not open his eyes, but he bent his head forward a little so that his forehead could rest against her hand. Thus they remained for several minutes. Then Scar came back, bringing a glass of milk, with the thick cream on it; he placed this on the table beside his father, climbed into his chair, and went on with his game, Bayard against Roland. The Major took the glass and began to sip the milk, at first critically, then appreciatively; he had the air of a connoisseur over a glass of old wine. "How is it this morning?" asked Madam Carroll, with interest. And she listened to his opinion, delivered at some length.

"I must go now," she said, rising; "Sara will be expecting me in the drawing-room."

She had taken off her gypsy hat and gloves, and put on a little white apron with blue bows on the pockets. As she crossed the room towards the door, with her bunch of household keys at her belt, she looked more like a school-girl playing at housekeeping than the wife of a man of the Major's age (or, indeed, of a man much younger than the Major), and the mother of Scar. But this was one of the charms among the many possessed by this little lady—she was so young and small and fair, and yet at the same time in other ways so fully "Madam Carroll" of "The Farms."

The Reverend Mr. Owen thought of this as she entered the drawing-room. He had thought of it before. The Reverend Mr. Owen greatly admired Madam Carroll.

When he had paid his visit and gone, Sara Carroll went up-stairs to her own room. She had her mantle on her arm, her bonnet in her hand, for she had not taken the trouble to go to her room before receiving his visit, as Madam Carroll had taken it: Madam Carroll always took trouble.

Half an hour later there was a tap upon her door, and her step-mother, having first waited for permission, entered. Sara had taken the seat which happened to be nearest the entrance, an old, uncomfortable ottoman without a back, and she still held her bonnet and mantle, apparently unconscious that she had them; the blinds had not been closed, and the

room was full of the noon sunshine, which struck
glaringly against the freshly whitewashed walls.
Madam Carroll took in the whole—the listless attitude, the forgotten mantle, the open blinds, the nearest chair. She drew the blinds together, making a
cool, green shade in place of the white light; then
she took the bonnet and mantle from the girl's pas-
sive hand, folded the mantle, and placed the two
carefully in the closet where they belonged.

"I can do that. You must not give yourself
trouble about my things, mamma," Sara said.

"It is no trouble, but a pleasure. I am so glad
to see other feminine things about the house; mine
have so long been the only ones—for I suppose we
can hardly count the neuter gowns of Judith Inches.
Don't you like the easy-chair Caleb and I made for
you?"

"It is very nice. I like it very much."

"But not enough to sit in it," said Madam Carroll, smiling.

"I really did not notice where I was sitting," said
the girl, getting up; "I almost always sit in the easy-
chair. But won't you take it yourself, mamma?"

"I would rather see you in it," answered Madam
Carroll. "Besides, it is too deep for me; there is
some difference in our lengths." She seated herself
in a low chair, and looked at the long, lithe shape

of Sara, opposite, her head thrown back, her slender feet out, her arms extended on the broad arms of the cushioned seat.

Sara, too, looked at herself. "I am afraid I loll," she said.

"Be thankful that you can," answered the smaller lady; "it is a most refreshing thing to do now and then. Short-backed women cannot loll. And then people say, 'Oh, *she* never rests! *she* never leans back and looks comfortable!' when how can she? It is a matter of vertebræ, and we do not make our own, I suppose. You did not stay long at Miss Dalley's. Didn't you find her agreeable?"

"She might have been—unaccompanied by Tasso."

Madam Carroll laughed. "He is her most intimate friend. She has quite taken him to her heart. She has been so anxious to see you, because you were acquainted with him in his own tongue, whereas she has been obliged to content herself with translations. She has a leaf from his favorite tree, and a small piece of cloth from his coat—or was it a toga? But no, of course not; doublet and hose, and those delightful lace ruffles which are such a loss to society. These valuable relics she keeps framed. It is really most interesting."

"I never cared much for Tasso," said Sara, indifferently.

"That is because you have had a large variety to choose from, reading as you do all the poets in the original, from Homer down to—to our sad but fascinating Lamartine," answered Madam Carroll, looking consideringly about the room, and finally staying her glance at the toilet-table, upon which she had expended much time and care. "But our poor Miss Dalley's life has been harshly narrowed down, narrowed, I may say, to Tasso alone. For all their small property was swept away by the war, and she is now obliged to support herself and her mother by dyeing: there is, fortunately, a good deal of dyeing in Far Edgerley, and so she took it up. You must have noticed her hands. But we always pretend not to notice them, because in all other ways she is so lady-like; when she expects to see any one, she always, and most delicately, wears gloves."

Madam Carroll related this little village history as though she were but filling an idle moment; but the listener received an impression, none the less, somewhere down in a secondary consciousness, that she had not quite done justice to poor Miss Dalley and her aspirations, and that some time she ought to try to atone for it.

But this secondary consciousness was small: it was small because the first was so wide and deep, and so filled with trouble — trouble composed in

equal parts of perplexity, disappointment, and grief.
She was at home, and she was not happy. This was
a conjunction of conditions which she had not believed could be possible.

She had never had any disagreements with her
father's wife, and she had been fond of her in a
certain way. But the wife had never been to the
daughter more than an adjunct—something added
to her father, of qualifying but not independent importance; a little moon, bright, if you pleased, and
pretty, but still a satellite revolving round its sun.
As a child, she had accepted the new mother upon
this basis, because she could make everything " more
pleasant for papa;" and she had gone on accepting
her upon the same basis ever since. Madam Carroll
knew this. She had never quarrelled with it. She
and her daughter had filled their respective positions
in entire amity. But now that this daughter had
come home to live, now that she was no longer a
school-girl or child, this was what she had discovered : her father, her idol, had turned from her,
and his wife had gained what his daughter had lost.
There could be no doubt but that he had turned from
her; his manner towards her was entirely changed.
He seemed no longer to care to have her with him;
he seemed to avoid her; he was not interested in
anything that was connected with her—he who had

formerly been so full of interest; he never kept
up a conversation with her, but let it drop as soon
as he could; he was so—so strange! Although she
had now been at home two weeks, she had scarcely
once been alone with him; Madam Carroll had either
been present from the beginning, or she had soon
come in; Madam Carroll had led the conversation,
suggested the topics. The Major had always been
fond of his pretty little wife; but he had also been
devoted to his daughter. The change in him she
could not understand; it made her very unhappy.
It would have made her more than that—made her
wretched beyond the possibility of concealment—
had there not been in it an element of perplexity;
perplexity which bewildered her, which she could
not solve. For, while her own position and her
father's regard for her seemed completely changed,
life at the Farms went on day after day upon the
distinct assumption that there was no change, that
everything was precisely as it always had been.
This assumption was not only mentioned, but insisted upon, the Major's wife often alluding with
amusement to what she called their "dear obstinate
old ways."

"The Major ties his cravat precisely as he did
twenty-five years ago—he has acknowledged it to
me," she said, glancing at him merrily. "We have

the same things for dinner; we wear the same clothes, or others made exactly like them ; we read the same books because we think them so much better than the new; we discuss the same old topics for the same prejudiced old reason. We remain so obstinately unchanged that even Time himself does not remember who we are. Each year when he comes round he thinks we belong to a younger generation."

The Major always laughed at these sallies of his wife. "You forget, my dear, my gray hairs," he said.

"Gray hairs are a distinction," answered Madam Carroll, decisively. "And besides, Major, they're the only sign of age about you; your figure, your bearing, are as they always were."

And on Sundays, when he carried round the plate at St. John's, and at his wife's receptions once in two weeks, this was true.

Sara came out of her troubled revery at the sound of Madam Carroll's voice. This lady was going on with her subject, as her step-daughter had not spoken.

"Yes, Caroline Dalley is really very intelligent; she is one of the subscribers for our *Saturday Review*. You know we subscribe for one copy—about twelve families of our little circle here—and it goes to all in turn, beginning with the Farms. The Major selected it; the Major prefers its tone to that of

our American journals as they are at present. Not
that he cares for the long articles. With his—his
wide experience, you know, the *long* articles could
only be tiresome; they weary him greatly."

"I must have tired him, then, this morning; I
read some of the long articles aloud."

"You had forgotten; you have been so long absent. It was very natural, I am sure. You will
soon recall those little things."

"How can I recall what I never knew? No,
mamma, it is not that; it is the—the change. I am
perplexed all the time. I don't know what to do."

"It isn't so much what to do as what not to do,"
replied Madam Carroll, looking now at the lounge
she had designed, and surveying it with her head a
little on one side, so as to take in its perspective.
"The Major has not yet recovered entirely from his
illness of last winter, you know, and his strength
cannot be overtaxed. A—a tranquil solitude is the
best thing for him most of the time. I often go
out of the room myself purposely, leaving him alone,
or with Scar, whose childish talk, of course, makes
no demand upon his attention; I do this to avoid
tiring him."

"I don't think *you* ever tire him," said Sara.

The Major's wife glanced at her step-daughter;
then she resumed her consideration of the lounge.

"That is because I have been with him so constantly. I have learned. You will soon learn also. And then we shall have a very happy little household here at the Farms."

"I doubt it," said the girl, despondently. She paused. "I am afraid I am a disappointment to my father," she went on, with an effort, but unable longer to abstain from putting her fear into words—words which should be in substance, if not in actual form, a question. "I am afraid that as a woman, no longer a school-girl or child, I am not what he thought I should be, and therefore whenever I am with him he is oppressed by this. Each day I see less of him than I did the day before. There seems to be no time for me, no place. He has just told me that all his mornings would be occupied; by that he must have meant simply that he did not want *me*." Tears had come into her eyes as she spoke, but she did not let them fall.

"You are mistaken," said Madam Carroll, earnestly. Then in her turn she paused. "I venture to predict that soon, very soon, you will find yourself indispensable to your father," she added, in her usual tone.

"Never as you are," answered Sara. She spoke with a humility which, coming from so proud a girl, was touching. For the first time in her life she was acknowledging her step-mother's superiority.

Madam Carroll rose, came across, and kissed her. "My dear," she said, "a wife has more opportunities than a daughter can have; that is all. The Major loves you as much as ever. He is also very proud of you. So proud, indeed, that he has a great desire to have you proud of him as well; you always have been extremely proud of him, you know, and he remembers it. This feeling causes him, perhaps, to make something of—of an effort when he is with you, an effort to appear in every respect himself, as he was before his illness—as he was when you last saw him. This effort is at times fatiguing to him; yet it is probable that he will not relinquish it while he feels that you are noticing or—or comparing. I have not spoken of this before, because you have never liked to have me tell you anything about your father; even as a child you always wanted to get your knowledge directly from him, not from me. I have never found fault with this, because I knew that it came from your great love for him. As I love him too, I have tried to please, or at least not to displease, his daughter; not to cross her wishes, her ideas; not to seem to her officious, presuming. Yet at the same time remember that I love him probably as much as you do. But now that you have asked me, now that I know you wish me to speak, I will say that if you could remove all necessity for the effort your father now makes, by placing yourself so fully upon a lower plane—if I may so express it—that his former self should not be suggested to him by anything in *you*, in your words, looks, or manner, you would soon find, I think, that this slight—slight constraint you have noticed was at an end. In addition, he himself would be more comfortable. And our dearest wish is of course to make him happy and comfortable, to keep him so."

As she uttered these sentences quietly, guardedly, Sara had grown very pale. Her eyes, large and dark with pain, were searching her step-mother's fair little face. But Madam Carroll's gaze was fixed upon the window opposite ; not until she had brought all her words to a close did she let it drop upon her daughter. Then the two women looked at each other. The girl's eyes asked a mute question, a question which the wife's eyes, seeing that it was an appeal to her closer knowledge, at length answered—answered bravely and clearly, sympathetically, too, and with tenderness, but—in the affirmative.

Then the daughter bowed her head, her face hidden in her hands.

Madam Carroll sat down upon the arm of the easy-chair, and drew that bowed head towards her. No more words were spoken. But now the daughter understood all. Her perplexity and her trouble were at an end; but they ended in a grief, as a river ends in the sea—a grief that opened out all round her, overwhelming the present, and, as it seemed to her then, the future as well. Madam Carroll said nothing; the bereavement was there, and the daughter must bear it. No one could save her from her pain. But the girl knew from this very silence, and the gentle touch of the hand upon her hair, that all her sorrow was comprehended, her desolation pitied, understood. For her father had been her idol, her all; and now he was taken from her. His mind was failing. This was the bereavement which had fallen upon her heart and life.

CHAPTER III.

At sunset of the same day Madam Carroll was in her dining-room; she had changed her dress, and now wore a fresh muslin, with a bunch of violets in her belt. Sara, coming down the stairs, saw the bright little figure through the open door; Judith Inches was bringing in the kettle (for Madam Carroll always made the tea herself), and on the table were one or two hot dishes of a delicate sort, additions to the usual meal. Sara recognized in these added dishes the never-failing touch of the mistress's hand upon the household helm. The four-o'clock dinner had come and gone, but no summons had been sent to her—that pitiless summons which in so many households remains inflexible, though stricken hearts may be longing for solitude, for a respite, however brief, from the petty duties of the day. Through the long hours of the afternoon there had been no knock, not so much even as a footstep outside her door. But now, in the cool of the evening, the one who had thus protected her seclusion was hoping that she would of her own accord come down and take again her accustomed place at the family table. Sara did this. She did more. She had put away the signs of her grief so completely that, save for an added pallor and the dark half-circle under her eyes, she was quite herself again. Her soft hair was smooth, her black dress made less severe by a little white scarf which encircled the narrow linen collar. Scar was sitting on the bottom stair as she came down. She put her hand on his head. "Where is papa?" she said.

"Papa is in the library. I think he is not coming out to tea," answered the child.

"Oh, but we must make him come—the dining-room is so dull without papa. Let us go and ask him." She took his hand, and they went together to the library. Madam Carroll, who had heard their words through the open door, watched them go. She did not interfere. She told Judith Inches to take back the hot dishes to the kitchen.

The Major was sitting in his easy-chair, looking at the pictures in an old book. He closed the volume and hastily drew off his spectacles as his daughter came in. "It has been a beautiful afternoon," he remarked, speaking promptly and decidedly. "Have you been out? or were you at home with a book—in your old way? What do you find to read nowadays? *I* find almost nothing." And he folded his arms with a critical air.

"I find little that can be compared with the old English authors, the ones you like," answered his daughter. "The old books are better than the new."

"So they are, so they are," replied the Major, with satisfaction. "I have often made the remark myself."

"Now that I am at home again," continued Sara, "I want to look over all those old books I used to have before I went to Longfields—those that were called mine. I hope we have them still?"

"Yes," said Scar, in his deliberate little voice, "we have. I read them now. And the long words I look out in the dictionary."

"It is a very good exercise for him. I suggested it," said the Major.

"I want to see all their old pictures again," pursued Sara. "I know I shall care a great deal about them; they will be like dear old friends."

"Very natural; I quite understand the feeling," said the Major, encouragingly. "And as Scar reads the books, perhaps you will find some of them lying about this very room. Let me see—didn't I have one just now? Yes, here it is; what was it?" And taking up the volume he had laid down a moment before, he opened it, and read, or repeated with the air of reading (for his spectacles were off), "'The

Life and Adventures of Robinson Crusoe and his Servant-man Friday. Defoe. London.'"

Sara came to his side and looked at the title-page. "Yes, that is my dear old book. I loved it better than any other, excepting, perhaps, 'Good Queen Bertha's Honey-Broth.' I wonder if the old pictures are all there?"

"I think they are," said the Major, turning the leaves. They looked at one or two together, recalling reminiscences of the days when she used to talk about them as a child. "You always insisted that this print of Friday's foot was not of the right shape, and once you even went out in the garden, took off your shoe and stocking, and made a print in a flower-bed to show me," said the Major, laughing.

"Let us look them all over after tea, and 'Good Queen Bertha' too," said Sara. "For Scar and I have come to take you out to tea, father; the dining-room is so dull without you. Besides, I want you to give me some peach preserves, and then say, 'No, Sara, not again,' when I ask for more; and then, after a few minutes, put a large table-spoonful on my plate with your head turned away, while talking to some one else, as though unconscious of what you were doing."

Scar laughed over this anecdote, and so did Scar's

father. "But perhaps we shall have no peach preserve," he said, rising.

"We will ask mamma to give us some," answered Sara. She took his arm, and Scar took his other hand; thus together they entered the dining-room.

Madam Carroll welcomed them; but placidly, as though the Major's coming was a matter of course. Since his daughter's return, however, it had not been a matter of course: first for this reason, then for that, his meals had almost always been sent to the library. Now he was tired; and now the dining-room floor might be damp after Judith Inches' scrubbing-brush; now there was an east wind, and now there was a west; or else he was not feeling well, and some one might "drop in," in which case, as the dining-room opened only into the hall, which was wide, like a room, he should not be able to escape. In actual fact, however, there was very little "dropping in" at Carroll Farms, unless one should give that name to the visits of the rector, Mr. Owen. Once in a while, in the evening, when the weather was decisively pleasant, the junior warden came to see them. But all their other acquaintances came to the receptions, made a brief call upon the first Thursday afternoon following, and that was all. The sweet little mistress of the mansion had never uttered one syllable upon the subject, yet each

member of the circle of Far Edgerley society knew
as well as though it had been proclaimed through
the town by a herald with a silver trumpet em-
blazoned with the Carroll arms, that these bimonth-
ly receptions (which were so delightful) and the brief
following call comprised all the visits they were expected to pay at Carroll Farms. And surely, when
one considered the great pleasure and also improve-
ment derived from these receptions, the four visits
a month at the Farms were worth more than forty
times four visits at any other residence in the village or its neighborhood. True, Mrs. Hibbard en-
deavored to maintain an appearance of importance
at her mansion of yellow wood called Chapultepec;
but as General Hibbard (of the Mexican War) had
now been dead eight years, and as his old house
had not been opened for so much as the afternoon
sewing society since his departure, its importance,
socially considered, existed only in the imagination
of his relict—which was, however, in itself quite a
domain.

Judith Inches, tall and serious, now brought back
the hot dishes, Madam Carroll made the tea (with
many pretty little motions and attitudes, which her
husband watched), and the meal began. The Major
was in excellent spirits. He told stories of Sara's
childhood, her obstinacy, her never-failing questions.

"She came to me once, Scar," he said, "and announced that Galileo was a humbug. When I asked
her why, she said that there was good King David,
who knew all about astronomy long before he did;
for didn't he say, ' the round world, and they that
dwell therein'? We sang it every Sunday. So that
proved plain as day that David knew that the world
was round, and that it moved, and all about it, of
course. Yet here was this old Italian taking everything to himself! Just like Amerigo Vespucci, an.
other old Italian, who had all America named after
himself, leaving poor Columbus, the real discoverer,
with nothing but ' Hail, Columbia!' to show for it.
She announced all this triumphantly and at the top
of her voice, from a window; for I was in the garden. When I told her that the word ' round,' upon
which all her argument had been founded, was not
in the original text, you should have seen how crest-
fallen she was. She said she should never sing that
chant again."

Scar laughed over this story. He did not laugh
often, but when he did, it was a happy little sound,
which made every one join in it by its merry glee.

"I am afraid I was a very self-conceited little
girl, Scar," his sister said.

As the meal went on, the Major's manner grew
all the time more easy. His eyes were no longer

restless. His old attention returned, too, in a meas-
ure ; he kept watch of his wife's plate to ask if she
would not have something more ; he remembered
that Sara preferred bread to the beat biscuit, and
placed it near her. The meal ended, they went back
to the library. Sara found her old copy of " Good
Queen Bertha's Honey - Broth," and she and her
father looked at the pictures together, as well as at
those of " Robinson Crusoe." Each had its associa-
tion, a few recalled by him, but many more by her.
After Scar had gone to bed, and the books had been
laid aside, she still sat there talking to him. She
talked of her life at Longfields, telling stories in
connection with it — stories not long — bright and
amusing. The Major's wife meanwhile sat near
them, sewing ; she sat with her back to the lamp, in
order that the light might fall over her shoulder
upon the seam. The light did the work she assigned
to it, but it also took the opportunity to play over
her curls in all sorts of winsome ways, to gleam on
her thimble, to glide down her rosy muslin skirt,
and touch her little slipper. She said hardly anything ; but, as they talked on, every now and then
she looked up appreciatively, and smiled. At last
she folded up her work, replacing it in her neat rose-
lined work-basket ; then she sat still in her low chair,
with her feet on a footstool, listening.

The old clock, with its fierce gilt corsair climbing over a glass rock, struck ten.

"Bed-time," said Sara, pausing.

"Not for me," observed the Major. "My time for sleep is always brief; five or six hours are quite enough."

"I remember," said his daughter. And the memory, as a memory, was a true one. Until recently the Major's sleep had been as he described it. He had forgotten, or rather he had never been conscious of, the long nights of twelve or thirteen hours' rest which had now become a necessity to him.

"I am afraid I am not like you, father. I am very apt to be sleepy about ten," said Sara. "And I suspect it is the same with mamma."

Madam Carroll did not deny this assertion. The Major, laughing at the early somnolence of the two ladies, rose to light a candle for his daughter, in the old way. As she took it, and bent to kiss her stepmother good-night, Madam Carroll's eyes met hers, full of an expression which made them bright (ordinarily they were not bright, but soft); the expression was that of warm congratulation.

The next day dawned fair and cloudless—Trinity Sunday. The mountain breeze and the warm sun together made an atmosphere fit for a heaven. On the many knolls of Far Edgerley the tall grass, car-

rying with it the slender stalks of the buttercups,
was bending and waving merrily ; the red clover,
equally abundant, could not join in this dance, because it had crowded itself so greedily into the de-
sirable fields that all that its close ranks could do
was to undulate a little at the top, like a swell passing over a pond. Madam Carroll, the Major, and
Scar were to drive to church as usual, in the equipage. Sara had preferred to walk. She started
some time before the hour for service, having a
fancy to stroll under the churchyard pines for a
while by herself. These pines were noble trees ;
they had belonged to the primitive forest, and had
been left standing along the northern border of the
churchyard by the Carroll who had first given the
land for the church a hundred years before. The
ground beneath them was covered with a thick carpet of their own brown aromatic needles. There
were no graves here save one, of an Indian chief,
who slept by himself with his face towards the west,
while all his white brethren on the other side turned
their closed eyes towards the rising sun. It was
a beautiful rural God's-acre, stretching round the
church in the old-fashioned way, so that the shadow
of the cross on the spire passed slowly over all the
graves, one by one, as the sun made his journey
from the peak of Chillawassee across to Lonely

Mountain, behind whose long soft line he always
sank, and generally in such a blaze of beautiful light
that the children of the village grew up in the vague
belief that the edge of the world must be just there,
that there it rounded and went downward into a
mysterious golden atmosphere, in which, some day,
when they had wings, they, too, should sport and
float like birds.

Early though it was, Miss Carroll discovered when
she entered the church gate that she was not the
first comer; the choir ladies were practising within,
and other ladies of floral if not musical tastes were
arranging mountain laurel in the font and chancel—
to the manifest disapproval of Flower, the disapproval being expressed in the eye he had fixed upon
them, his " mountain eye," as he called his best one.
" It be swep, and it be dustered," he said to himself.
" What more do the reasonless female creatures
want ?" Miss Carroll had not joined the choir, although the rector, prompted by his junior warden,
had suggested it; Miss Sophia Greer would, therefore, continue to sing the solos undisturbed. She
was trying one now. And the other ladies were
talking. But this music, this conversation, this arrangement of laurel, and this disapproval of Flower
went on within the church. The new-comer had the
churchyard to herself; she went over to the pines

on its northern side, and strolled to and fro at the
edge of the slope, looking at the mountains, whose
peaks rose like a grand amphitheatre all round her
against the sky.

Her face was sad, but the bitterness, the revolt,
were gone; her eyes were quiet and sweet. She had
accepted her sorrow. It was a great one. At first
it had been overwhelming; for all the brightness
of the past had depended upon her father, all her
plans for the present, her hopes for the future. His
help, his comprehension, his dear affection and interest, had made up all her life, and she did not know
how to go on without them, how to live. Never
again could she depend upon him for guidance,
never again have the exquisite happiness of his perfect sympathy—for he had always understood her,
and no one else ever had, or at least so she thought.
She had cared only for him, she had found all her
companionship in him; and now she was left alone.

But after a while Love rose, and turned back this
tide. The sharp personal pain, the bitter loneliness,
gave way to a new tenderness for the stricken man
himself. Evidently he was at times partly conscious
of this lethargy which was fettering more and more
his mental powers, for he exerted himself, he tried
to remember, he tried to be brighter, to talk in the
old way. And who could tell but that he perceived

his failure to accomplish this? Who could tell,
when he was silent so often, sitting with his eyes on
the carpet, that he was not brooding over it sadly?
For a man such as he had been, this must be deep
suffering—deep, even though vague—like the sensation of falling in a dream, falling from a height, and
continuing to fall, without ever reaching bottom.
Probably he did not catch the full reality; it constantly eluded him; yet every now and then some
power of his once fine mind might be awake long
enough to make him conscious of a lack, a something that gave him pain, he knew not why. As she
thought of this, all her heart went out to him with
a loving, protecting tenderness which no words could
express; she forgot her own grief in thinking of his,
and her trouble took the form of a passionate desire
to make him happy; to keep even this dim consciousness always from him, if possible; to shield
him from contact with the thoughtless and unfeel-
ing; to so surround his life with love, like a wall,
that he should never again remember anything of
his loss, never again feel that inarticulate pain, but
be like one who has entered a beautiful, tranquil garden, to leave it no more.

This morning, under the pines, she was thinking
of all this, as she walked slowly to and fro past the
Indian's grave. Flower came out to ring his first

bell. His "first bell" was unimportant, made up of
short, business-like notes ; he rang it in his working
jacket, an old mountain homespun coat, whose swal-
low-tails had been cut off, so that it now existed as
a roundabout. But when, twenty minutes later, he
issued forth a second time, he was attired in a coat
of thin but shining black, with butternut trousers
and a high pink calico vest. Placing his hat upon
the ground beside him, he took the rope in his hand,
made a solemn grimace or two to get his mouth into
position, and then, closing his eyes, brought out with
gravity the first stroke of his "second bell." His
second bell consisted of dignified solo notes, with
long pauses between. Flower's theory was that each
of these notes echoed resonantly through its following pause. But as the bell of St. John's was not one
of size or resonance, he could only make the pauses
for the echoes which should have been there.

As the first note of this second bell sounded from
the elm, all the Episcopal doors of Far Edgerley
opened almost simultaneously, and forth came the
congregation, pacing with Sunday step down their
respective front paths, opening their gates, and proceeding decorously towards St. John's in groups of
two or three, or a family party of father, mother,
and children, the father a little in advance. They
all arrived in good season, passed the semi-uncon-

scious Flower ringing his bell, and entered the church.
Next, after an interval, came "clatter," "clatter:"
they knew that "the equipage" was coming up
the hill. Then "clank," "clank:" the steps were
down.

All now turned their heads, but only to the angle
which was considered allowable—less than profile,
about a quarter view of the face, with a side glance
from one eye. To them, thus waiting, now entered
their senior warden, freshly dressed, gloved, carrying his hat and his large prayer-book; and as he
walked up the central aisle, a commanding figure,
with noble head, gray hair, and military bearing, he
was undoubtedly a remarkably handsome, distin-
guished-looking man.

Behind him, but not too near, came the small figures of Madam Carroll and Scar, the lady in a simple summer costume of lavender muslin, with many
breezy little ruffles, and lavender ribbons on her
gypsy hat, the delicate hues causing the junior warden to exclaim (afterwards) that she looked like "a
hyacinth, sir; a veritable hyacinth!" Scar, in a
black velvet jacket (she had made it for him out of
an old cloak), carrying his little straw hat, held his
mother's hand. The Major stopped at his pew,
which was the first, near the chancel; he turned,
and stood waiting ceremoniously for his wife to

enter. She passed in with Scar; he followed, and they took their seats. Then the congregation let its chin return to a normal straightness, the bell stopped, Alexander Mann (to use his own expression) "blew up," and Miss Millie began.

Miss Carroll came in a minute or two late. But there was no longer much curiosity about Miss Carroll. It was feared that she was "cold;" and it was known that she was "silent;" she had almost no "conversation." Now, Far Edgerley prided itself upon its conversation. It never spoke of its domestic affairs in company; light topics of elegant nature were then in order. Mrs. Greer, for instance, had Horace Walpole's Letters—which never failed. Other ladies preferred the cultivation of flowers, garden rock-work, and their bees (they allowed themselves to go as far as bees, because honey, though of course edible, was so delicate). Mrs. Rendlesham, who was historical, had made quite a study of the characteristics of Archbishop Laud. And the Misses Farren were greatly interested in Egyptian ceramics. Senator Ashley, among many subjects, had also his favorite; he not infrequently turned his talent for talking loose upon the Crimean War. This was felt to be rather a modern topic. But the junior warden was, on the whole, the most modern man they had. Too modern, some persons thought.

CHAPTER IV.

JULY passed, and August began. Sara Carroll had spent the weeks in trying to add to her father's comfort, and trying also to alter herself so fully, when with him, that she should no longer be a burden upon his expectation, a care upon his mind. In the first of these attempts she was and could be but an assistant, and a subordinate one, filling the interstices left by Madam Carroll. For the Major depended more and more each day upon his little wife. Her remarks always interested him, her voice he always liked to hear; he liked to know all she was doing, and where she went, and what people said to her; he liked to look at her; her bright little gowns and sunny curls pleased his eye, and made him feel young again, so he said. He had come, too, to have a great pride in her, and this pride had grown dear to him; it now made one of the important ingredients of his life. He liked to mention what a fine education she had had; he liked to say that her mother had been a " Forster of Forster's Island," and that her father was an Episcopal clergyman who had "received his education at Oxford." He thought little Scar had "English traits," and these he enumerated. He had always been a proud man, and now his pride had centred itself in her. But if his pride was strong, his affection was stronger; he was always content when she was in the room, and he never liked to have her long absent. When he was tired, she knew it; he was not obliged to explain. All his moods she comprehended; he was not obliged to define them. And when he did appear in public, at church on Sundays, or at her receptions, it was she upon whom he relied, who kept herself mentally as well as in person by his side, acting as quick-witted outrider, warding off possible annoyance, guiding the conversation towards the track he preferred, guarding his entrances and exits, so that above all and through all her other duties and occupations, his ease and his pleasure were always made secure.

Of all this his daughter became aware only by degrees. It went on so unobtrusively, invisibly almost, that only when she had begun to study the subject of her father's probable needs in connection with herself, what she could do to add to his comfort, only then did she comprehend the importance of these little hourly actions of Madam Carroll, comprehend what a safeguard they kept all the time

round his tranquillity, how indispensable they were
to his happiness. For the feeling he had had with
regard to his daughter extended, though in a less
degree, to all Far Edgerley society ; he wished—and
it was now his greatest wish—to appear at his best
when any one saw him. And, thanks to the devotion and tact of his wife, to her watchfulness (which
never seemed to watch), to the unceasing protection
she had thrown round his seclusion, and the quiet
but masterly support she gave when he did appear,
no one in the village was as yet aware that any
change had come to the Major, save a somewhat
invalid condition, the result of his illness of the preceding winter.

Sara herself had now learned how much this opinion of the Far Edgerley public was to her father ;
he rested on Saturday almost all day in order to
prepare for Sunday, and the same preparation was
made before each of the receptions. At these receptions she could now be of use ; she could take
Madam Carroll's place from time to time, stand beside him and keep other people down to his topics,
prevent interruptions and sudden changes of subject, move with him through the rooms, as, with
head erect and one hand in the breast of his coat,
he passed from group to group, having a few words
with each, and so much in the old way that when

at length he retired, excusing himself on account of his health, he left unbroken the impression which all Far Edgerley cherished, the impression of his distinguished appearance, charming conversation, and polished, delightful manners.

During these weeks, the more his daughter had studied him and the ways to make herself of use to him, even if not a pleasure, the greater had become her admiration for the little woman who was his wife—who did it all, and so thoroughly! who did it all, and so tenderly! What she, the daughter, with all her great love for him, could think out only with careful effort, the wife divined; what she did with too much earnestness, the wife did easily, lightly. Her own words when she was with him were considered, planned; but the wife's talk flowed on as naturally and brightly as though she had never given a thought to adapting it to him; yet always was it perfectly adapted. Sara often sat looking at Madam Carroll, during these days, with a wonder at her own long blindness; a wonder also that such a woman should have borne always in silence, and with unfailing gentleness, her step-daughter's moderate and somewhat patronizing estimate of her. But even while she was thinking of these things Madam Carroll would perhaps rise and cross the room, stopping to pat dog Carlo on the rug as she passed, and

she would seem so small and young, her very prettiness so unlike the countenance and expression one
associates with a strong character, that the daughter
would unconsciously fall back into her old opinion
of her, always, however, to emerge from it again hur-
riedly, remorsefully, almost reverentially, upon the
next example of the exquisite tact, tenderness, and
care with which she surrounded and propped up her
husband's broken days.

But the Major's life was now very comfortable.
His daughter, if she had not as yet succeeded in
doing what she did without thought over it, had, at
least, gradually succeeded in relieving him from all
feeling of uneasiness in her society: she now came and
went as freely as Scar.   She had made her manner so
completely unexpectant and (apparently) unobserv-
ant, she had placed herself so entirely on a line with
him as he was at present, that nothing led him to
think of making an effort; he had forgotten that
he had ever made one.   She talked to him on local
subjects, generally adding some little comment that
amused him; she had items about the garden and
fields or dog Carlo to tell him; but most of all she
talked to him of the past, and led him to talk of it.
For the Major had a much clearer remembrance of
his boyhood and youth than he had of the events of
later years, and not only a clearer remembrance, but

a greater interest; he liked to relate his adventures of those days, and often did it with spirit and zest. He was willing now to have her present at "Scar's lessons;" she formed sentences in her turn from the chivalrous little manuscript book, and took part in the game of dominoes that followed. The Major grew into the habit also of taking an afternoon walk with her about the grounds—always at a safe distance from the entrance gate. They went to visit the birds' nests she had discovered, and count the eggs or fledglings, and he recalled his boyhood knowledge of birds, which was clear and accurate; they went down to the pond made by the brook, and sent in dog Carlo for a bath; they strolled through the orchard to see how the apples were coming on, and sat for a while on a bench under the patriarch tree. These walks became very precious to the daughter; her father enjoyed them, enjoyed so much the summer atmosphere, pure and fresh and high, yet aromatic also with the scents from the miles of unbroken pine and fir forest round about, enjoyed so much looking at the mountains, noting the moving bands of light and shadow cast upon their purple sides as the white clouds sailed slowly across the sky, that sometimes for an hour at a time he would almost be his former self again. He knew this when it happened, and it made

him happy. And Sara was so glad to see him happy
that she began to feel, and with surprise, as if she
herself too might be really happy again, happy after
all.

This first little beginning of happiness grew and
budded like a flower; for now more and more her
father asked for her, wanted her with him; he took
her arm as they walked about the grounds, and she
felt as glad and proud as a child because she was
tall enough and strong enough to be of real use to
him. She remembered the desolation of those hours
when she had thought that she should never be of
use to him again, should have no place beside him,
should be to him only a care and a dread; thinking
of this, she was very thankfully happy. When she
could do something for him, and he was pleased, it
seemed to her almost as if she had never loved him
so much ; for, added to her old strong affection, there
was now that deep and sacred tenderness which fills
the heart when the person one loves becomes dependent—trustingly dependent, like a little child—
upon one's hourly thought and care.

The rector of St. John's had continued those visits which Miss Carroll had criticised as too frequent.
When he came he seldom saw his senior warden ;
but the non-appearance was sufficiently excused by
the state of the senior warden's health, as well as

made up for by the presence of his wife. For Madam Carroll was charming in her manner to the young clergyman, always giving him the kind of welcome which made him feel sure that she was glad to see him, and that she wished him to come again. As he continued to come, it happened now and then that the mistress of the house would be engaged, and unable to see him. Perhaps she was reading to the Major from his *Saturday Review;* and this was something which no one else could do in the way he liked. She alone knew how to select the items he cared to hear, and, what was more important, how to leave the rest unread; she alone knew how to give in a line an abstract that was clear to him, and how to enliven the whole with gay little remarks of her own, which, she said, he must allow her—a diversion for her smaller feminine mind. The Major greatly valued his *Saturday Review;* he would have been much disturbed if deprived of the acquaintance it gave him with the events of the day. Not that he enjoyed listening to it; but when it was done and over for that week, he had the sensation of satisfaction in duty accomplished which a man feels who has faced an east wind for several hours without loss of optimism, and returned home with a double appreciation of his own pleasant library and bright fire. One's life should not be too per-

sonal, too easy; there should be a calm consideration
of public events, a general knowledge of the outside
world—though that outside world, tending as it did
at present too much towards mere utilitarian inter-
ests, was not especially interesting; thus spoke the
Major at the receptions (with that week's *Saturday* fresh in his memory), as he alluded briefly to
the European news. For they never discussed American news at the receptions; they never came farther
westward, conversationally, than longitude twenty-
five, reckoned, of course, from Greenwich. In 1868
there was a good deal of this polite oblivion south
of the Potomac and Cumberland.

When, therefore, Mr. Owen happened to call at a
time when Madam Carroll was engaged, Miss Carroll was obliged to receive him. She did not dislike him (which was fortunate; she disliked so many
people!), but she did not care to see him so often,
she said. He talked well, she was aware of that; he
had gone over the entire field of general subjects
with the hope, as it seemed, of finding one in which
she might be interested. But as she was interested
in nothing but her father, and would not talk of
him now, save conventionally, with any one, he
found her rather unresponsive.

His congregation thought her, in addition, cold.
Not a few of them had mentioned to him this opin-

ion. But there was something in Sara Carroll's face which seemed to Owen the reverse of cold, though he could not deny that to him personally she was, if not precisely wintry, at least as neutral as a late October day, when there is neither sun to warm nor wind to vivify the gray, still air. Yet he continued to come to the Farms. His liking for the little mistress of the house was strong and sincere. He thought her very sweet and winning. He found there, too, an atmosphere in which he did not have to mount guard over himself and his possessions—an atmosphere of pleasant welcome and pleasant words, but both of them unaccompanied by what might have been called, perhaps, the acquisitiveness which prevailed elsewhere. No one at the Farms wanted him or anything that was his, that is, wanted it with any tenacity; his time, his thoughts, his opinions, his approval or disapproval, his ideas, his advice, his personal sympathy, his especial daily guidance, his mornings, his evenings, his afternoons, his favorite books, his sermons in manuscript—all these were considered his own property, and were not asked for in the large, low-ceilinged drawing-room where the Major's wife and daughter, one or both, received him when he came. They received him as an equal (Miss Carroll as a not especially important one), and not as a superior, a being from another world; though Madam

Carroll always put enough respect for his rector's position into her manner to make him feel easy about himself and about coming again.

He continued to come again. And Miss Carroll continued her neutral manner. The only change, the only expression of feeling which he had seen in her in all these weeks, was one look in her eyes and a sentence or two she had uttered, brought out by something he said about her mother. During one of their first interviews he had spoken of this lady, expressing, respectfully, his great liking for her, his admiration. Madame Carroll's daughter had responded briefly, and rather as though she thought it unnecessary for him to have an opinion, and more than unnecessary to express one. He had remembered this little passage of arms, and had said no more. But having met the mistress of the house a few days before, at a cabin on the outskirts of the town, where a poor crippled boy had just breathed his last breath of pain, he had been much touched by the sweet, comprehending, sisterly tenderness of the mother who was a lady to the mother who was so ignorant, rough-spoken, almost rough-hearted as well. But, though rough-hearted, she had loved her poor child as dearly as that other mother loved her little Scar. The other mother had herself said this to him as they left the cabin together. He spoke of it to

Sara when he made his next visit at the Farms; he could not help it.

And then a humility he had never seen there before came into her eyes, and a warmth of tone he had not heard before into her voice.

"My mother's goodness is simply unparalleled," she answered. "You admire her sincerely; many do. But no one save those who are in the house with her all the time can comprehend the one hundredth part of her unselfishness, her energy—which is always so quiet—her tenderness for others, her constant thought for them."

Frederick Owen was surprised at the pleasure these words gave him. For they gave him a great pleasure. He felt himself in a glow as she finished. He thought of this as he walked home. He knew that he admired Madame Carroll; and he was not without a very pleasant belief, too, that she had a respect for his opinion, and even an especial respect. Still, did he care so much to hear her praised?—care so much that it put him in a glow?

Towards the last of August occurred, on its regular day, one of Madame Carroll's receptions. To Sara Carroll it was an unusually disagreeable one. She had never been fond of the receptions at any time, though of late she had accepted them because they were so much to her father; but this particular one was odious.

7

It was odious on account of the presence of a stranger who had appeared in Far Edgerley three weeks before, a stranger who had made his way into society there with so much rapidity and success that he had now penetrated even the exclusive barriers of the Farms. But this phraseology was Miss Carroll's. In reality, the stranger's " way" had not been made by any effort of his own, but rather by his manners and appearance, which were original, and more especially by a gift for which nature was responsible, not himself. And as to " penetrating the barriers" of the Farms, he had not shown any especial interest in that old-fashioned mansion, and now that he was actually there, and at one of the receptions, too, he seemed not impressed by his good fortune, but wandered about rather restlessly, and yawned a good deal in corners. These little ways of his, however, were considered to belong to the " fantasies of genius ;" Madam Carroll herself had so characterized them.

The stranger had, indeed, unlimited genius, if signs of this kind were to be taken as evidences of it; he interrupted people in the middle of their sentences; he left them abruptly while they were still talking to him ; he yawned (as has already been mentioned), and not always in corners; he went to see the persons he fancied, whether they had asked him to do so or not; he never dreamed of going to see the persons he did not fancy, no matter how many times they had invited him. He had a liking for flower-gardens, and had been discovered more than once, soon after his arrival, sitting in honeysuckle arbors which the owners had supposed were for their own private enjoyment. When found, he had not apologized; he had complimented the owners upon their honeysuckles.

Strangers were so rare in Far Edgerley—high, ancient little village in the mountains, far from railways, unmentioned in guide-books—that this admirer of flower-gardens was known by sight through all the town before he had been two days in the place. He was named Dupont, and he was staying at the village inn, the Washington Hotel—an old red brick structure, whose sign, a weather-beaten portrait of the Father of his Country, crowned the top of a thick blue pole set out in the middle of Edgerley Street. He was apparently about twenty-eight or thirty years of age, tall, slender, carelessly dressed, yet possessing, too, some picturesque articles of attire to which Far Edgerley was not accustomed; notably, low shoes with red silk stockings above them, and a red silk handkerchief to match the stockings peeping from the breast pocket of the coat; a cream-colored umbrella lined with red silk; a quantity of cream-colored gauze wound round a straw hat.

But it was not these articles, remarkable as they were, nor his taste for opening gates without permission, nor his habit of walking in the middle of the street, ignoring sidewalks, nor another habit he had of rising and going out of church just before the sermon—it was none of these which had given him his privilege of entering "the best society." The best society had opened its doors to Genius, and to Genius alone. This genius was of the musical kind. Dupont played and sang his own compositions. "What," said Madam Carroll, "is genius, if not this?"

Madam Carroll's opinion was followed in Far Edgerley, and Dupont now had the benefit of it. The Rendleshams invited him to tea; the Greers sang for him; he was offered the *Saturday Review;* even Mrs. General Hibbard, joining the gentle tide, invited him to Chapultepec, and when he came, showed him the duck yard. Miss Honoria Ashley did not yield to the current. But then Miss Honoria never yielded to anything. Her father, the junior warden, freely announced (outside his own gate) that the "singing man" amused him. Mr. Phipps hated him, but that was because Dupont had shown some interest in Miss Lucy Rendlesham, who was pretty. Not that they cared much, however, for beauty in

Far Edgerley ; it was so much better to be intellectual. Ferdinand Kenneway, when he learned that the new-comer had been received both at Chapultepec and the Farms, called at the inn, and left one of his engraved cards — "Mr. F. Kenneway, Baltimore." He had once lived in Baltimore six months. Dupont made an excellent caricature of Ferdinand on the back of the card, and never returned the call. On the whole, the musician had reason to congratulate himself upon so complete a conquest of Far Edgerley's highest circle. Only two persons (besides Phipps) in all that circle disliked him. True, these two disliked him strongly; but they remained only two, and they were, in public, at least, silent. They were Miss Carroll and the rector of St. John's.

Perhaps it was but natural that a clergyman should look askance at a man who always rose and walked out of church at the very moment when he was preparing to begin his sermon. Miss Carroll, however, had no such sufficient reason to give for her dislike; when Dupont came to the Farms he was as respectfully polite to her as he could be in the very small opportunity she vouchsafed him. He came often to their flower-garden. She complained of his constant presence. "I am never sure that he is not there. He is either lying at full length in the shade of the rhododendrons, or else sitting in the rose arbor, drumming on the table."

" Very harmless amusements they seem to me," replied Madam Carroll.

" Yes. But why should we be compelled to provide his amusements? I think that office we might decline."

" You are rather unkind, aren't you? What harm has the poor fellow done to us?"

" Oh, if you are going to pity him, mamma—"

" Why should not one pity him a little?—a young man who is so alone in the world, as he tells us he is, not strong in health, and often moody. Then, too, there is his genius."

" I am tired of his genius. I do not believe in his genius. There is no power in it. Always a ' little song!' A ' little song!' His little songs are too sweet; they have no force."

" Do you wish him to shout?"

" I wish him to take himself elsewhere. I am speaking freely, mamma; for I have noticed that you seem to like him."

" He is a variety — that is the explanation; we have so little variety here. But I do like him, Sara, or, rather, I like his songs. To me they are very beautiful."

Nothing more was said on either side. Sara had

"HE CAME OFTEN TO THEIR FLOWER GARDEN."

announced her dislike, and it had been ignored; her regard for Madam Carroll kept her from again expressing the feeling.

The present reception was considered an especially delightful one. One reason for this was that Madam Carroll had altered her hours; instead of from five to eight, they were now from eight to ten. True, the time was shorter; but this was compensated for by the change from afternoon to evening. For choice as had been the tone of elegant culture which had underlain these social meetings heretofore, there was no doubt but that they gained in the element of gayety by being deferred to candle-light. The candles inspired everybody; it was felt to be more festal. The ladies wore flowers in their hair, and Ferdinand Kenneway came out in white gloves. The Major, too, had not appeared so well all summer as he did this evening; every one remarked it. Not that the Major did not always appear well. "He is, and always has been, the first gentleman of our state. But to-night, how peculiarly distinguished he looks! His gray hair but adds to his noble appearance—don't you think so?—his gray hair and his wounded arm? And dear Madam Carroll, too, when have you seen her look so bright?"

Thus the ladies. But the daughter of the house, meanwhile, had never been more silent. To-night

she merited, without doubt, their adjective " cold."
She had not been able to be of much use to her
father this evening. During the three quarters of
an hour he had given to his guests Madam Carroll
had not left him; together they had gone through
the rooms, exchanging greetings, holding short con-
versations, inquiring after the health of the absent.
As had been remarked, the little wife looked very
bright. She had more color than usual; her complexion had never had, they said, a more exquisite
bloom. She was dressed in white, with a large bunch
of pink roses fastened in her belt, and as she stood
by the side of her tall, gray - haired husband she
looked, the junior warden declared, like " a Hebe."
And then he carefully explained that he meant an
American Hebe of delicate outlines, and not the
Hebe of the ancient Greeks—" who always weighed
two hundred."

The American Hebe talked with much animation;
Far Edgerley admired her more than ever. After
the Major had retired she was even gay; the junior
warden having lost the spray of sweet-pea from his
button-hole, with charming sportiveness she called
him to her and replaced it with one of her pink
roses.

Meanwhile Mr. Dupont was conducting himself
after his usual fantasied fashion. He strolled about

and leaned against the walls—a thing never done in Far Edgerley, on account of the paper; he stared at the head-dress of Mrs. General Hibbard, an impressive edifice of black lace and bugles; he talked a little to Miss Lucy Rendlesham, to the rage of Phipps; he turned his back on F. Kenneway; and he laughed at the poetical quotations of Mrs. Greer. And then he made no less than six profound bows before Miss Corinna, the dignified leader of St. John's choir.

He bowed whenever he met her, stopping especially for the purpose, drawing his feet together, and bending his head and body to an angle heretofore unwitnessed in that community. Miss Corinna, in chaste black silk, became at last, martial though she was, disconcerted by this extreme respect. She could not return it properly, because, most unfortunately, as she had always thought, the days of the courtesy, the only stately salutation for a lady, were gone by. She bowed as majestically as she could. But when it came to the seventh time, she said to her second sister, " Really, Camilla, his attentions are becoming too pressing. Let us retire." So they retired—to the wall. But even here they were not secure, Dupont discovering their retreat, and coming by expressly every now and then to bestow upon the stately maiden another salute.

Towards the end of the evening—or rather, of the

reception—he sang, accompanying himself upon the
guitar. His guitar had a long loop of red ribbon
attached to it; Miss Carroll surveyed it and its
owner with coldest eye, as, seated upon a low ottoman in the centre of the room, he began what she
had called his " little songs." His songs were, in
truth, always brief; but they were not entirely
valueless, in spite of her prejudice against them.
They had a character of their own. Sometimes they
contained minor strains too old for Far Edgerley to
remember, the wild, soft, plaintive cadences of the
Indian women of tribes long gone towards the set-
ting sun, of the first African slaves poling their flat-
boats along the Southern rivers. And sometimes
they were love-songs, of a style far too modern for
the little, old-fashioned town to comprehend. Dupont's voice was a tenor, not powerful, but delicious-
ly, sensuously sweet. As he sat there singing, with
his large, bold dark eyes roving about the room, with
his slender dark fingers touching the strings, with
his black moustache, waxed at the ends, the gleam of
his red handkerchief, and the red flower in his coat,
he seemed to some of the ladies present romantically
handsome. To Sara Carroll he seemed a living impertinence.

What right had this person of unknown antece-
dents, position, and character to be posturing there

before them?—to be admitted at all to the house of
her father? And then her eyes happened to fall
upon her father's wife, who, in the chair nearest the
musician, was listening to him with noticeable enjoyment. She turned and left the room.

By doing this she came directly upon Frederick
Owen, who had apparently performed the same action a little while before. They were alone in the
wide hall; every one else was in the drawing-room,
gathered round the singer.

"It—it was cooler here," Owen explained, rather
awkwardly. At this instant Dupont's voice floated
out to them in one of his long, soft notes. "It has
'a dying fall,' has it not?" said the clergyman; he
was trying to speak politely of her guest. But as
his eyes met those of Miss Carroll, he suddenly read
in them a feeling of the same strength and nature
as his own, regarding that guest. This was a surprise, and a satisfaction. It was the first corresponding dislike he had been able to discover. For his
own dislike had been so strong that he had been
searching in all directions for a corresponding one,
with the hope, perhaps, of proving to himself that
his was not mere baseless prejudice. But until this
evening he had not succeeded in finding what he
sought. It was all the other way.

It should be mentioned here that Owen had not

betrayed this dislike of his. If he had done so, if
his objection to the musician had been known, or
even suspected, it is probable that Dupont would
hardly have attained his present position in Far
Edgerley. For after Madam Carroll's opinion, the
opinion of the rector of St. John's came next. But
he had not betrayed it. There was nothing of essen-
tial importance against Dupont. The fact that he
was precisely the kind of fellow whom Frederick
Owen particularly disliked was simply a matter between the two men themselves, or rather, as Dupont
cared nothing about it, between Owen and his own
conscience ; for he could hardly go about denounc-
ing a man because he happened to play the guitar.
But after three weeks of enduring him—for he met
him wherever he went — it was great comfort to
have caught that gleam of contempt in Miss Carroll's fair gray eyes ; he was glad that he had been
at just the right spot in the hall to receive it as she
came from the drawing-room with that alluring
voice floating forth behind her.

"It is a beautiful evening," he said, dropping
the subject of the musician ; "the moonlight is so
bright that one can see all the mountains. Shall
we go out and look at them ?"

And Miss Carroll was so displeased with the scene
within that she consented to withdraw to the scene

without; and there they remained as long as the singing lasted. They walked up and down the broad piazza; he talked about the mountain scenery, and the waterfalls. She did not appear to be much interested in them. Her companion, however, was not so much chilled by this manner of hers as he had sometimes been; he had had a glimpse behind it.

CHAPTER V.

EARLY in the week following the reception, Frederick Owen learned that Dupont was about to take
his departure from Far Edgerley, and with no expectation of returning. This was good news. He was
beginning to have the feeling that the fellow would
never go away, that he and his guitar would become
a permanent feature of Madam Carroll's receptions,
his lounging figure under the cream-colored umbrella
a daily ornament of the centre of Edgerley Street.
Was he really, then, going? It seemed too good to
be true. But the tidings had been brought by Miss
Dalley, who was both good and true, and who was
accurate as well; she had the very hour—" On Friday, at nine."

" Hangman's day !" thought Owen, with satisfaction, doing his thinking this time with the remnants
of boyhood feelings; for though he was in his third
decade—the beginning of it—and a clergyman, the
boy in him was by no means entirely outgrown.
Miss Dalley had come to return a book, Longfellow's

"Outre Mer," and to borrow anything he might have about Ferrara.

"I was so much interested in our American poet's description of the Italian poet's grave, on the Janiculum," she said. "It was such a touching passage, and it contained this truly poetical sentence: 'He sleeps midway between his cradle at Sorrento and his dungeon at Ferrara.' I can never go in *person*, Mr. Owen; Fate has denied me that. But I can think of the inscription, which Longfellow gives: 'Torquati Tasso ossa hic jacet,' and be there in *mind*."

She had called it "hic jacket." "Jacent, I think," said the rector, gently.

"Yes, certainly; that is what I meant—jacinth," said Miss Dalley, correcting herself. "A beautiful word, is it not? And so appropriate, too, for a poet's grave, mentioned, as it is, in Revelations!"

On Friday Dupont really did go. The rector himself saw him pass in the high red wagon of the Washington Inn on his way down the mountain to the lower town, the eastward-bound stage, and thence —wherever he pleased, the gazer thought, so long as he did not return. But although the rector gave this vagueness to the musician's destination, it was understood in other quarters that he was going back to the West India Islands—"where he used to live, you know."

"Upon which one did he live?" asked the junior warden. "There are about fifty thousand of them, large and small; he can't have lived on them all."

"For my part, I think him *quite* capable of it," answered Miss Honoria, grimly.

Having seen the musician depart, Owen jumped on his horse and went off to one of his mission stations far up among the crags of Lonely Mountain. For, not content with a rector's usual duties, all of which he attended to with a modern promptness unknown in the days of good old Parson Montgomery, he had established mission stations at various points in the mountains above Far Edgerley. Wherever there were a few log-houses gathered together, there he held services, or started a Sunday-school. He was by far the most energetic rector the parish of St. John in the Wilderness had ever had; so much so, indeed, that the parish hardly knew how to take his energy, and thought that he was perhaps rather too much in the wilderness — more than necessity demanded or his bishop required. Miss Honoria Ashley had even called these journeyings of his "itinerant;" but Miss Honoria was known to disapprove, on general principles, of everything the rector did: she had once seen him wearing a sack-coat.

On this particular Friday he was out all day among the peaks, close up under the sky. Coming down at

sunset, and entering Edgerley Street, with its knolls
and flower-gardens and rambling old houses, his
home seemed to him a peaceful and pleasant one.
And then, as he passed Carroll Farms, he became
conscious that the cause for its seeming especially
peaceful to him this evening was the absence of the
intruder, that man from another world, who was no
longer there to contaminate its sweet, old-fashioned
simplicity with his dubious beauty, his dangerous
character, and his enchanting voice. For Owen believed that the musician's character was dangerous;
his face bore the marks of dissipation, and though
indolent, and often full of gay good-nature, he had
at times a reckless expression in his eyes. Nothing
deterred him from amusing himself; and probably,
in the same way, nothing would deter him from any
course towards which he should happen to feel an
inclination. He was not dangerous by plan or cal-
culation; he was dangerous from the very lack of
them. He was essentially erratic, and followed his
fancies, and no one could tell whither they would
lead him. But he might have been all this, and the
clergyman would still have felt able to guard his
parish and people from any harm his presence might
do them, had it not been for the favor shown him
by Madam Carroll. This had been a blow to Owen.
He said to himself that the gentle lady's love of

music had blinded her judgment, and carried her
astray. It was a satisfaction that Miss Carroll's
judgment remained unblinded. But it was greatest
satisfaction of all that the man was gone; he con-
gratulated himself upon this anew as he rode by the
gateway of the Farms.

It was well that he had this taste of comfort. It
did not last long. Less than three weeks had passed
when he learned one afternoon that Dupont had
returned. And not long afterwards he was in possession of other knowledge, which troubled him
more than anything that had happened since he
came to Far Edgerley.

In the meantime his parish, unaware of its rector's opinion, had welcomed back the summer visitor
with various graceful little attentions. The summer
visitor had been seriously ill, and needed attentions,
graceful or otherwise. He had journeyed as far as
New York, and there had fallen ill of a fever, which
was not surprising, the parish thought, when one
considered the dangerously torrid climate of that
business metropolis at this season. Upon recovery,
he had longed with a great longing for "our pure
Chillawassee air," and had returned to pass the time
of convalescence "among our noble peaks;" this
was repeated from knoll to knoll. Dupont's appearance bore testimony to the truth of the tale. He

had evidently been ill: his cheeks were hollow, and he moved about slowly, as though he had not much strength; his eyes, large and dark, looked larger and darker than ever, set in his thin, brown face. But he was still Dupont; his moustache was still waxed, and he had some new articles of finery, a gold watch-chain, and a seal-ring on his long-fingered hand. This time he did not stay at the inn; he preferred to try a farm-house, and selected Walley's Cove, a small farm a little above the village, in one of the high ravines which, when wide enough for a few fields along the mountain-brook that flowed through the centre, were called coves. Dupont liked the place on account of the view; and also, he said, because he could throw a stone from the cove's mouth "into every chimney in Far Edgerley." This was repeated. "Do you suppose," said Mrs. General Hibbard, solemnly—"do you suppose he is going to do it?"

This lady had felt from the beginning a solemn curiosity about Dupont, about all he said and did. But this was quite natural, the village thought, when one considered the interesting proximity of the West India Islands (where the musician used to live) to the glorious Mexican field of her departed husband's fame. But, in return for her interest, Dupont had irreverently made a caricature of the august widow, depicting her as a mermaid, in her own duck-pond, surrounded by all her ducks, clad in Mexican costumes; and then Far Edgerley society, which had been obliged to listen for eight long years to many details about these birds of Chapultepec—Far Edgerley society was corrupt enough to laugh.

But this incident belonged to Dupont's first visit; and, like other incidents of his first visit, could be deemed amusing or impertinent according to one's view of him. The new knowledge which had come to Frederick Owen was something very different— different and grave: Sara Carroll had changed. She now felt an interest in this stranger, and she was showing it.

Was this the influence of Madam Carroll? But Owen could not long think this. Miss Carroll was not a person to be easily influenced or led. She was not yielding; whatever course she might follow, one could at least be sure that, good or bad, it was her own. Her interest showed itself guardedly; so much so that no one had observed it. The clergyman felt sure that he was the only discoverer, and his own discovery he owed to a rare chance. He was coming down Chillawassee on horseback, and in bending to gather a flower from a bush, as he passed, he had lost a small note-book from the breast pocket of his coat; dismounting to look for it, he found that it was lying on a ledge not far below the road, and that he could get it by a little climbing. He made his way down to the ledge, and secured the book. Then he saw, a little farther down, one of the isolated rocks called chimneys, and was seized with the fancy to have a look from its top. He obeyed this fancy. And from its top he found himself looking directly down into a small field on the edge of Carroll Farms; here, standing together under a tree, were two figures which he instantly recognized —they were the figures of Sara Carroll and Dupont. This field was separated from the road by a hedge so high that no one could look over it, and from the other fields and the orchard of the Farms by a thicket of chincapins. The two were therefore well hidden; they were safe from discovery save for the remote chance that some one had climbed the chimney above them. And this one remote chance had fallen to the lot of Frederick Owen.

He was much surprised, uncertain, unhappy. Shielded by the tall bushes growing on top of the chimney, he had stood for several minutes looking down upon the two. Then he left the rock, went back to his horse, and rode home.

His uneasiness, after spoiling his night's sleep, took him to the Farms the next afternoon. Madam Carroll received him in the drawing-room. She offered an excuse for Miss Carroll; it seemed that she had a headache. But on his way out the clergyman distinctly saw the shadow of a man thrown across the dining-room floor by the bright sunshine shining through the western windows. It might not be the shadow of Dupont, of course; he was ashamed of himself for his quick suspicion. It might be that of some other visitor, or of one of their poor pensioners, or of Caleb Inches. But no masculine visitor came to the Farms at this hour save, now and then, the junior warden, whose small figure never cast shadow like that; and all the pensioners of whom he had knowledge were women. He decided that, of course, it was Inches; and then, on his way down Carroll Lane, he met Inches coming up. Still, it was but a supposition. He forced himself to cast it aside.

Chance, however, seemed determined to disturb him, for she soon threw in his way other knowledge, and this not a shadow, but reality. He caught a glimpse of Sara Carroll turning into a little - used path, which led up the mountain to a fir-wood. His own road (he was on horseback, as usual, on his way to a mission station) led him by Walley's Cove, and here, fifteen minutes later, he distinctly saw the figure of Louis Dupont entering the same wood at its upper edge, and by the path which would bring him directly to her, the same path she herself was following.

Owen's trouble now took complete possession of him; up to this time he had fought it off. He felt that he ought to do something, to act. Dupont was a dissipated, erratic adventurer, whose history no one knew. Should he let this proud, fastidious, delicate-minded girl fall into such a vulgar trap as this? Before his eyes, within reach of his hand? Yet there it was again—if she were in reality as proud and fastidious as he had supposed her to be (and he had thought her the proudest girl he had ever known), how could she, of her own accord, endure Louis Dupont? At one time she had not endured him. There had been a memorable moment when the expression of her eyes (how well he remembered it!) had been unmistakable; the moment when he had met her, coming from the drawing-room, with that alluring voice floating forth behind her. What could have changed her — changed her so completely as this?

The one answer presented itself with pitiless promptness: Dupont had changed her. He had accomplished it himself, with the aid of a handsome face, fine eyes, and an audacity which stopped at nothing; for the clergyman had always felt sure that the audacity was there, although it had not, in

Far Edgerley, at least, been much exerted. This
was so acutely disagreeable to the man who was
thinking of it, that there was in his own eyes (handsome ones, too, in their way—a blue way) angry
moisture as he went over its possibilities.   He
clinched his hand and rode on; it would have fared
hardly with the musician had he crossed his path
just then.   Owen was a clergyman.   But he had
been a man, and a free one, first; he had not gone
from college and seminary directly into the minis-
try.   He was thirty-one years old, and he had taken
orders but two years before; the preceding interval
had not been spent in country villages.

   With all this surging feeling, however, he had as
yet nothing definite against this stranger—this
stranger whose bad manners had been protected by
his "genius," and whose bad aspects had not been
perceived by the innocent little town.   By nothing
definite he meant nothing that he could use.   But
now Chance, having given him three heavy burdens
of knowledge to carry (he had carried them as well
as he could, with a heavy heart as well)—the knowledge of those three meetings which, if not clandestine, were at least concealed—this same Chance
relented so far as to present him with other knowledge—knowledge of a different hue.   She put in his
possession some recent facts concerning the musi-

cian which were proof, and proof positive, against him.

But what could Owen do with his facts? If he had not known what he knew of Sara Carroll's interest in him, he could have proceeded against the fellow at once; it needed but the statement which he was now able to make to close every door in Far Edgerley against him, for the little town, though not strait-laced, had a standard of morals as pure as its own air. But if he should do this, might not Dupont take his revenge, or, less than that, amuse himself, as he would call it, by letting the village public learn of his intimate relations with the Farms, or rather with Miss Carroll? Madam Carroll's liking for him, or, rather, for his songs, was known and comprehended. But Miss Carroll's liking was not known; and it had, too, an aspect—and here Frederick Owen felt that he would rather go on forever in silence than have that aspect discussed. Yet something he must do. He decided to go to Major Carroll himself. Infirm as was his health, and secluded as was his life, he was the natural protector of these two ladies, and would wish to know, ought to know, everything that concerned them. He went to the Farms.

The Major was not feeling well that day; Madam Carroll hoped that the rector would excuse him.

The rector had no alternative but to do so. He asked if he might not see him on the following day. Madam Carroll, with regret, feared that this would not be possible; he had taken cold, and his colds always lasted for a long time; he had not yet recovered his strength fully after that illness of the preceding winter—as the rector was probably aware. Disappointed, the rector went away. As he passed down green Edgerley Street he met Dupont coming up, as usual, in the centre of the roadway. The musician gave the clergyman a profound bow, almost as profound as those with which he had disconcerted Miss Corinna. As Owen returned it—as slightly as possible—he thought he saw in Dupont's eyes a mocking gleam of amusement. Amusement? Or was it triumph? He went on his way, walking rapidly; but at a certain point in the road he could not help looking back. Yes, Dupont had turned into Carroll Lane.

On the next day the rector of St. John's, having taken a new resolution, started to pay a morning visit at the residence of his senior warden. In answer to his knock Judith Inches opened the door. Without waiting for words from him, this guardian of the Farms announced that the Major was not well, and that the ladies were engaged, and would like to be excused. She then seemed quite prepared to close the door.

"Perhaps Madam Carroll would see me, if she knew it was I," said Owen.

Judith Inches thought there was no probability of this.

The tall, blue-eyed man on the door-step did not accept her probability; he suggested that she at least make it sure.

Judith surveyed him from head to foot; then, gradually, as much of a smile as ever illumined her countenance stole across its lean, high-cheek-boned expanse; she beckoned him in, and pointed with a long forefinger down the hall towards a half-open door. "*Miss Sara's* theer," she said.

It was the door of the dining-room. Visitors were not invited to enter this room, save at the receptions, and Owen, after advancing a step or two, stopped; the permission of Judith Inches seemed hardly enough.

And then this mountain maid, in her lank brown gown, drew near, and murmured in his ear these mystic words: "Go right along in. What yer feared of? I've noticed that you was feared of her before now. *That's* no way. Brace up, man, brace up. Stiffen in an irun will, and you'll do it." She then softly and swiftly withdrew down the hall, turning to give him a solemn wink at a far door before she disappeared.

Owen felt a great schoolboy blush rising all over his face as he stood there alone. Had the feminine eye of this serious spinster discovered what he himself had not? But no; he always knew all about himself. She had simply discovered, woman-fashion, more than existed. He went down the hall, and entered the dining-room. There, at its western window, sat Sara Carroll, sewing.

She answered his greeting, and gave him her hand. "I heard a knock, but there was so long a delay that I supposed no one had entered," she said.

He took a seat, explaining that Judith Inches had told him to come to this room. "My visit is more especially to either Major or Madam Carroll this morning," he said. "But your tall handmaiden was sure that they would not be able to receive me."

"My father is not well to-day, and mamma has a headache. Judith was right," answered Miss Carroll. She took up her sewing again, and went on with the seam.

Owen, who had brought himself up to the point of speaking to Madam Carroll herself (for he had no hope, after yesterday, of seeing the Major), was disappointed. It was a difficult task he had undertaken, and he wanted to do it, and have it over. Foiled for this day at least, he still sat there, his eyes on Miss Carroll's moving needle. He was thinking a little, perhaps, of Judith Inches' remarkable imagination; but far more of Miss Carroll herself. Her delicately cut face, with its reserved expression, was there before him. Yet this was the same girl who had received Dupont in this very room, who had talked with him in that secluded meadow, who had gone to the fir-wood to meet him. His eyes showed his inward trouble, they looked bluely dense and clouded. Miss Carroll glanced at him once or twice, as it seemed to him, guardedly; but he was aware that he was no longer a calm judge where she was concerned; aware that he might easily mistake the importance or significance of any little look or act. He fell into almost complete silence, so that she was obliged to find topics herself, and keep up the conversation; heretofore, when with her, this had always been his task.

He had sat there twenty minutes when there was a light step in the hall, and Madam Carroll entered. She came towards him with her hand extended and a smile of welcome. "Why did they not tell me you were here, Mr. Owen? It was by mere chance that I happened to hear the sound of your voice, and came down."

Sara had risen as her mother entered, her work dropping to the floor. "Oh, mamma!" she mur-

mured.   Then, "I have told Mr. Owen that you
have a headache," she explained.

"A mere trifle.   And it is over now.   Besides,
headache or no headache, I always wish to see
Mr. Owen," said the Major's wife, giving him her
hand.

Owen tried to recall his prearranged sentences, and
summoned all his coolness and skill.   The opportunity he had sought was to be his after all; now
let him use it to the best advantage.   But it was
not easy to tell a lady in her own house that both
her taste and her judgment had been at fault.

"I especially wished to see you this morning,
Madam Carroll," he said; "I am very glad you
came down.   I am anxious to speak with you upon
a subject which seems to me important."

"I am at your service," answered the lady, giving
the ruffle of her overskirt a pat of adjustment, and
then drawing forward a low willow chair.

"I think—I think, with your permission, we will
go to another room," said the clergyman.

Miss Carroll was still standing; she made no of-
fer to go.   Again she looked at their visitor, and
this time it seemed to him that it was more than
guardedly, that it was defiance.   "Mamma," she
said, "with your headache—for I know you have
it still—are you not undertaking too much?   Mr.

Owen will excuse you. Or could I not take your place?" And she turned to Owen.

"No," he answered; "you could not." And he said no more. He was aware that he was proceeding clumsily, but he could not help it. He found that he cared too much about it to do it gracefully or with skill. He recalled her slender, black-robed figure going towards the fir-wood, and his eyes grew more clouded than before. He turned away. "Of course, if Madam Carroll is suffering," he said —then he stopped; he did not want to postpone it again.

Madam Carroll threw up her hands. "My dear Sara, you make so much of my poor little headache that Mr. Owen will think I am subject to headaches. But I am happy to say that I am not; as a general thing, they are mere feminine affections. Come to the drawing-room, Mr. Owen. At this hour we shall not be interrupted." She led the way thither, and seated herself in her favorite chair, having first rolled forward a larger one for her guest. The spindle-legged furniture of the old-fashioned room had been covered by her own deft fingers with chintz of cream-color, enlivened with wreaths of bright flowers; over the windows and doors hung curtains of the same material. In this garden-like expanse Owen took his seat, collected himself and what he

9

had to say in one quick moment of review, and then began.

First, he asked her to pardon what was, in one way, the great liberty he was taking in speaking at all; in excuse he could only say that it seemed to him important — important to her own household. And in no household the world held had he a deeper, a more sincere, interest than in her own.

Madam Carroll begged to recall to his remembrance that that was saying a great deal — "no household in the world."

He did not answer this little speech, archly made. He took up his main subject. He told her that he had been unwilling to speak to her of it at all; that he should have greatly preferred speaking to the Major; but that had not been possible, at least for the present, as she was aware. The matter concerned itself with some facts he had lately learned about a person who had been generally received in Far Edgerley and also at the Farms—a person of whose history they really knew nothing, this—this musician—

" Are you pretending you do not know his name ?" asked Madam Carroll. " I can tell you what it is if you have forgotten ; it will make your story easier: Dupont—Louis Eugene Dupont."

Owen was astounded by her manner ; he had never seen anything like it in her before. Her large blue eyes

—of a blue lighter than his own—looked at him calmly, almost, it seemed to him, with a calm impertinence.

"I had not forgotten his name," he answered, gravely. "I have had too much reason to remember it. He has given me anxiety for some time past, Madam Carroll. I have felt that he was not the person to be received among us as he has been received. We are rather a secluded mountain village, you know, and there has been little here to tempt him into betraying himself; but I have suspected him from the first, and now—"

"You are rather inclined to suspect people, aren't you?" said Madam Carroll, with the same calm gaze.

"Major Carroll would have suspected him also had he ever met him."

"As it happens, my husband has met him. It was at one of our receptions; early in the evening, I think, before you came."

"And he said nothing?"

"Nothing."

"I must go on in any case," said Owen; "I can do no otherwise. For it is not for my own sake I am speaking—"

"Are you sure of that?" said his hostess, interrupting him again without ceremony. This time her tone had an amusement in it, an amusement not unmixed with sarcasm.

"I should do it just the same though I were on the eve of leaving Far Edgerley forever, never expecting to see any of you again," he answered, with some heat.

"It could hardly be a final parting, even then ; for the world is not so large as you suppose, Mr. Owen. It hardly seems necessary, on the whole, to be so tragic," answered the lady, again adjusting the ruffle of her overskirt, and laughing a little.

Owen was bewildered. He had thought that he knew her so well, he had thought that she was of all his parish his best and kindest friend; yet there she sat, within three feet of him, looking at him mockingly, turning all his earnest words into ridicule, laughing at him.

He was no match for her in little sarcasms, and he was in no mood for that kind of warfare. He said no more about himself and his feelings; he simply gave her a plain outline of the facts which had recently come into his possession.

Madam Carroll replied that she did not believe them. Such stories were always in circulation about handsome young men like Louis Dupont. They were told by other men—who were jealous of them.

Owen, who had grown a little pale, quietly gave her his proofs. The scene of the affair was one of his own mission stations—the most distant one ; he knew the young girl's father, and even the young girl herself.

"Oh, it seems *you* knew her too, then," said Madam Carroll, laughing. "I suppose she liked Dupont best."

The young clergyman was struck into silence. This little, gentle, golden-haired lady, whom he had admired so long and so sincerely, was this she? Were those her words? Was that her laugh? It seemed to him as if some evil spirit had suddenly taken up his abode in her, and having driven out her own sweet soul, was looking at him through her pretty eyes, and speaking to him with her pretty, rose-leaf lips. Stinging, under the circumstances insulting, as had been her speech, he was not angry; he was too much grieved. He could have taken her in his arms and wept over her. For what could it all mean save that Dupont had in some way obtained such control of her, poor little woman, that she was ready to attack everybody and anybody who attacked him?

He looked at her, still in silence. Then he rose. "I have told you all I know, Madam Carroll," he said, sadly, taking his hat from the chair beside him. "I had hoped that you would— I never dreamed that you could receive me or speak to me in the way you have. I have had the greatest regard for you; I have thought you my best friend."

Madam Carroll had also risen, with the air of wishing to close the interview. She dropped her eyes as he said these last words, and lifted her handkerchief to her mouth.

"I think as much of you as ever," she murmured. And then she began to cough, a cough with a long following breath that was almost like a sob.

The door opened, and Sara Carroll entered. She came straight to her mother, and put her arm round her as if to support her. "I knew you were not well, mamma. Mr. Owen will certainly excuse you *now*." And she looked at their guest with a glance which he felt to be dismissal.

Madam Carroll, exhausted by the cough, leaned against her daughter, her face covered by her handkerchief. Owen turned to go. But when he saw the daughter standing there so near him, when he thought of what he knew of her interest in this man, and of the mother's recent tone about him, his heart failed him. He could not go — go and leave her without one word of warning, one effort to save her, to show her what he felt.

"I came to warn Madam Carroll against Louis Dupont," he said, abruptly. "Madam Carroll has not credited what I have said, or, rather, she is not impressed by it. Yet it is all true. And probably there is much more. He is not a person with whom you should have intimate acquaintance, or, indeed, any acquaintance. As Madam Carroll will not do so, will you let *me* warn you?"

Miss Carroll started slightly as he said this. Then she recovered herself. "Surely it is nothing to me," she said, indifferently, with a slight emphasis on the "me."

Owen watched the indifferent expression. "She is acting," he thought. "She does it well!" Then aloud, "On the contrary, I suppose it to be a great deal to you," he answered, his eyes, intent and sorrowful, fixed full upon her over the little mother's head.

Madam Carroll took down her handkerchief, and the two women faced him with startled gaze. Sara was calm; but Madam Carroll's eyes, at first only startled, were now growing frightened. She turned her small face towards her daughter dumbly, as if for help.

The girl drew her mother more closely to her side. "And what right have you to suppose anything?" she said to Owen, with composure. "Are you our guardian?"

"Would that I were!" answered Owen, with deepest feeling in his tone. "I don't 'suppose' anything, Miss Carroll—I know. I have been unfortunate enough to see you with this man, or going to

meet him, and it has made me wretched. But do
not be troubled—no one else has seen it, and with
me you are perfectly safe; I would guard you with
my life. I had intended to expose him; I am in
possession of some facts which tell heavily against
him (Madam Carroll knows what they are); but
now how can I, when I fear that he—when I know
that you—" he paused; his voice was trembling a
little, and he wished to control the tremor.

"And if I should tell you that there was no occasion for either your fears or your advice?" said Sara
Carroll, after a moment's silence. She raised her
eyes again, and met his gaze steadily. "If I should
tell you that Mr. Dupont—to whom you object so
strongly—had the right to be with me as much as
he pleased, and that I had given him this right,
surely you would then understand that your warning came quite too late, and that both your opinion
and your advice were superfluous? And you would,
perhaps, spare us further conversation on a matter
that concerns only ourselves."

"Am I to believe this?" said Owen.

"You have it from me directly—I don't know
what better authority you would have. I tell you
in order to show you, decisively, that further inter-
ference on your part will be unnecessary. It is a
secret as yet, and, for the present, we wish it to re-

"THE GIRL DREW HER MOTHER MORE CLOSELY TO HER SIDE."

main one; we trust to you not to betray it. And I
think you will now keep to yourself, will you not,
what you know, or fancy you know, against him?"
She looked at him inquiringly.

"If I could only have seen your father!" said
Owen, with bitterest regret.

Her face changed, her arm dropped from her
mother's shoulders; she turned abruptly from him.

Left alone, Madam Carroll straightened herself, as
if trying to resume her usual manner. She looked
after Sara, who had crossed the broad room to a
window opposite. Then she looked at Owen. She
came closer to him. "I am sure it will not last, this
—this engagement of hers," she said, in a whisper,
shielding her lips with her hand as if to make her
tone still lower. "It is only a little fancy of the
moment, you know, a fancy founded upon his genius,
his musical genius, and his lovely voice. But it will
pass, Mr. Owen; I am sure it will pass. And in the
meantime our course—yours and mine—should be
just *silence*. Everything must go on as usual, and
you must say nothing against him to any one; that
is the most important of all. No one has suspected
it but you. She *has* been rather incautious; but I
will see that that is mended, so that no one else shall
suspect. If we are careful and silent, Mr. Owen,
you and I—the only ones who know—and if we

simply have patience and *wait*, all will yet be well; I assure you all will yet be well." She smiled, and looked up anxiously into his face with her soft blue eyes; she was quite her gentle self again.

"She is protecting her husband's daughter to the extent of her power," thought the young man, who was listening; "that has been the secret of her enigmatical manner from the beginning." But while he thought this, he was frowning with the pain her words had given him—a "fancy of the moment"—Louis Dupont!

"Promise me to say nothing against him," continued Madam Carroll, in the same earnest whisper, still smiling anxiously, and looking up in his face.

"Of course I shall say nothing. How could I do otherwise now?" answered Owen. "But my trouble is as great as ever, and my fear. You do not comprehend him, Madam Carroll. You do not see what he really is."

"Oh, I comprehend him—I comprehend him," said Madam Carroll, in a strained though still whispering tone. "I do my best, Mr. Owen," she added, in a broken voice—"my very best."

These last words were uttered aloud. Sara Carroll left the window and came back to her mother; she took her hands in hers. "Kindly excuse us now," she said to the clergyman, with quiet dignity.

He bowed, and left the room, his face still full of trouble and pain. They heard him close the front door behind him.

"I think he will say nothing," said Sara.

Madam Carroll had drawn her hands away; she stood motionless, looking at the carpet.

"Yes, it is safe now; don't you think so?" Sara continued, musingly.

Her step-mother raised her eyes. There was a flash in them. "I bore it because I had to. But it was the hardest thing of all to bear. You despise him, you know you do. You always have. You have been pitiless, suspicious, cruel."

"Not lately, mamma," said the girl. She put her arms round the little figure, and, with infinite pity, drew it towards her. Madam Carroll at first resisted; then the tense muscles relaxed, and she let her head rest against her daughter's breast. The lashes fell over her bright, dry eyes.

"You will never be able to keep it up," she murmured, after a moment, her eyes still closed.

"Yes, I shall, mamma."

"Never, never."

"I could do a great deal more for my dear father's sake," answered the girl, after a short hesitation.

Madam Carroll began to sob. "I have been a

good wife to him, Sara," she murmured, appeal-
ingly, piteously.

"Indeed you have, mamma. You are all his happiness, all his life; he could not live without you.
But you ought to rest; let me go with you up-stairs."

"I must go alone," answered Madam Carroll. She
had repressed her sobs, but her breath still came and
went unevenly. "It is not that I am angry, Sara;
do not think that. I was—but it has passed; I am
quite reasonable now—as you see. But, for a little
while, I must be alone, quite alone."

She left the room with her usual quick, light step.
After she had gone, Sara stood for a few moments
with her hands clasped over her eyes. Then she
went to the library.

Scar was playing dominoes, Roland against Bayard; and the Major was watching the game. His
daughter bent her head, and kissed his forehead;
then she sat down beside him, holding his hand in
hers, and stroking it tenderly.

"Well, my daughter, you seem to think a good
deal of me to-day," said the old man, smiling.

"Not only to-day, but always, papa—always," answered the girl, with emotion.

"Roland is very dull this morning," said the Major, explaining the situation. "He has lost three
games, and is going to lose a fourth."

CHAPTER VI.

FAR EDGERLEY was deprived of its rector. Mr. Owen had gone to the coast to attend the Diocesan Convention. But as he had started more than a week before the time of its opening, and had remained a week after its sessions were ended, Mrs. General Hibbard was of the opinion that he was attending to other things as well. She had, indeed, heard a rumor before he came that there was *some one* (some one in whom he felt an interest) elsewhere. Now it is well known that there is nothing more depressing for a parish than a rector with an interest, large or small, "elsewhere." St. John in the Wilderness was therefore much relieved when its rector returned, with no signs of having left any portion of himself or his interest behind him. And Mrs. General Hibbard lost ground.

Mr. Owen had started eastward on the day after his interview with the two ladies of Carroll Farms; he had started westward on the day after the arrival of a letter from his junior warden. This letter, written in a clear, old-fashioned hand, decorated with much underscoring, was a mixture of the formal phraseology of the warden's youth and that too-modern lightness which he had learned in his later years, and of which Miss Honoria so justly disapproved. He was supposed to be writing about church business. Having finished that (in six lines), he added an epitome of the news of the whole village, from the slippers which Miss Sophy Greer, at the north end of Edgerley Street, was working for him (the rector) — ecclesiastical borders, with the motto "Vestigia nulla retrorsum"—down to the last new duck in the duck-pond at Chapultepec, the south end of it. Among the items was this: "That amusing fellow Dupont is, I am sorry to say, ill, and I suspect seriously. It is a return of the fever he had in New York, I am told. He is at the Cove, and the Walleys are taking care of him. It has leaked out " ("leaked out "—oh, poor Miss Honoria!) "that he has no money, not even enough to pay for his medicines—those musicians are always an improvident lot, you know. But our lovely Madam Carroll, ministering angel that she is, pitying lady of the manor, has supplied everything that has been necessary. I have just heard, as I write these lines, that the poor fellow is no better."

The rector, upon his return, busied himself in attending to the many duties which had accumulated during his absence. He did not go to the Farms immediately; but as he was making no calls for the present—owing to the accumulation—the omission was not noticed. The musician was very ill, and every one was sorry. His poverty was now generally known; but Madam Carroll was doing all that was needful, and the poor wanderer lacked nothing. That was what they called him now—the "poor wanderer;" it was a delicate way of phrasing the fact that he was without means. Far Edgerley people were as far as possible from being mercenary; they had no intention of turning their backs upon Dupont because he was poor. They were poor themselves, and, besides, that had never been the Southern way. They would gladly have helped him now, had there been opportunity, and they looked forward to helping him as far as they were able so soon as he should have recovered his health. But at present Madam Carroll was doing the whole, and the whole was only—could be only—a doctor and medicines.

In all this there was nothing of Sara; that secret, the rector perceived, had been carefully kept. There was nothing, too, of the recent evil story concerning the musician, which he had related to Madam Carroll. But he had been aware that if he himself

10

should be silent, it was probable that nothing of it would reach Far Edgerley, at least for some time. For the mission station was remote, and the mountain people were very proud in their way, proud and reticent. They had, too, an opinion of Far Edgerley which was not unlike the opinion Far Edgerley had of the lower town. Pride in these mountains seemed a matter of altitudes. Owen knew that he was glad that these two hidden things had remained undiscovered; that, at least, was clear in the conflicting feelings that haunted his troubled heart.

He had returned on Monday evening; the week passed and Sunday dawned without his having seen any of the Carrolls. They came to church as usual; that is, the Major came, with his wife and little Scar; Miss Carroll was absent. After service the Major waited. The Major always waited. He waited to speak to his rector; it was a little attention he always paid. Owen knew that he was waiting, knew that he was standing there at the head of the aisle in his military attitude, with his prayer-book under his arm; yet, although he knew it, it was some minutes before he came forth. When at length he did appear, the Major advanced, shook hands with him, and asked how he was. The rector replied that he was quite well.

"Mr. Owen is probably the better for his journey," said Madam Carroll, joining her husband in the open space at the foot of the chancel steps, where the two men were standing. "A journey is always so pleasant, and especially a journey to the coast."

"Ah, yes," said the Major; "your journey. I hope you enjoyed it?"

"The coast is considered so beneficial," continued Madam Carroll. "For my own part, however, I prefer our mountain air; it seems to me more bracing. And the Major thinks so too."

"Certainly," said the Major; "I have often made the observation." He said a few words more, shook hands with the rector a second time, bowed, and then offered his arm to his wife. She took it, with a farewell smile to the rector, and they went down the aisle together through the empty church towards the open door. And Owen, who had been looking forward with eagerness, yet at the same time with dread, to his first meeting with Miss Carroll or her mother, found himself almost able to smile over the contrast between his own inward trouble and pain and the smiling self-possession of the little lady of the Farms. There rose before him her strange manner during the beginning of that last morning interview in her drawing-room; and then her frightened face turned towards her daughter; and then

her effort to excuse to him that daughter's avowal.
But in thinking of all this, he soon lost himself in
thoughts of the daughter alone. This was not a
new experience ; he forced his mind to turn from
the haunting subject, in active preparations for the
duties of the afternoon.

In the meantime the Major and his wife had
reached the porch. Scar was waiting for them outside, sitting on a little tombstone in the sunshine,
and a number of Far Edgerley people were standing about the gate. The Major bowed to these with
much courtesy, and Madam Carroll with much grace ;
they entered their carriage, Inches folded up the
steps, climbed to his perch, the mules started, and
" the equipage " rolled away.

They reached home ; but, in getting out, the bearing of the Major was not quite so military as it had
been at the church door. Inches came to his as-
sistance, and he took his wife's arm, and kept it
until he was in his own easy-chair again in the
library. There he sat all the afternoon. His wife
—for she did not leave him—read aloud to Scar,
and heard him recite his little Sunday lessons. Then
she took him on her lap and told him Bible stories,
speaking in a low tone, as the Major was now asleep.
They were close beside him, mother and little son.
The child's face was a curious mixture of her deli-

cate rose-tinted prettiness and the bold outlines of his father.

The sun, which had been journeying down the western sky, now touched the top of Lonely Mountain, and immediately all its side was robed in purple velvet, and its long summit tipped with gold. Still farther sank the monarch; and now he was out of sight. Then rose such a splendor of color in the west that it flooded even this quiet room across the valley, turning the old paper on the walls into cloth of gold, and Scar's flaxen hair into a little halo. The Major was now awake; he moved his easy-chair to the open window in order to see the sunset. Scar got another chair, climbed up, and sat down beside him. "I think, papa," he said, after some moments of silence, during which he had meditatively watched the glow — "I think it very probable that the little children who have to die young live over in that particular part of heaven. For those beautiful colors would amuse them, you know; and they must be very lonely up in the sky, without their fathers and mothers."

"Fathers and mothers die too, sometimes, my boy," answered the Major, his eyes turning misty. He took Scar's little hand, and held it in his own.

His wife came up behind him and laid her hand on his shoulder. The old Major looked up at her as

she stood by his chair, with a great trust and affection in his dim glance. For of late the Major had
been growing older rapidly; his eyes were losing
their clearness of vision; there were now many
sounds he could not hear. But he always heard
every intonation of her voice; always saw the hue
of her dress, and any little change in its arrangement. Where she was concerned, his dulled senses
were young again.

"My sister Sara is coming," announced Scar. "I
can see her. I can see the top of her bonnet above
the hedge, because she is so tall." And soon the
girl's figure appeared in sight. She opened the gate,
and came up the path towards the front door. Scar
leaned forward and waved his hand. She returned
his greeting, looking at the group of three in the
window—father, mother, and child.

The Major could not see his daughter, but he
turned his face in the direction of the path and gave
a little bow and smile. "She has been gone a long
time," he said to his wife; "almost all day."

His wife did not reply; she had left the room.
She met Sara in the hall. "I have come back for
you, mamma," whispered the girl. "I think the
time has come."

"I will go immediately," said Madam Carroll,
walking quickly towards the stairs. Then she

stopped. "But how can I? You would have to go with me. And at this hour the Major would notice it. He would notice it if we should both leave him. It would trouble him." She looked at Sara as she stood uttering these sentences. Though her voice was quiet, the suffering in her eyes was pitiable to see.

"Go, mamma. For this one time do not mind that. Judith will be here."

"No," answered Madam Carroll, with the same measured utterance; "the Major must not be troubled, his comfort must always be first. But as he is generally tired on Sunday evenings, perhaps he will go to bed early. I must wait, in any case, until he is asleep."

"Mamma, you cannot bear it," urged Sara, following her.

"Instead of saying that, you should tell me if there is hope—hope that I may not be too late," said Madam Carroll almost sternly, putting aside the girl's outstretched hands.

"I think he may not—they said he would not—Mrs. Walley said, 'He will pass at dawn,'" answered Sara, using the mountain phrase.

"I may then be in time," said Madam Carroll, in the same calm voice. She turned the handle of the door. "You had better join us soon. Your father has been asking for you." She went in, closing the door behind her.

When Sara entered, fifteen minutes later, she found her singing the evening hymn to the Major. The Major liked to have her sing that hymn on Sunday evenings, and Scar liked it too, because he could join in with his soft little alto.

> "The day is past and gone,
>   The evening shades appear;
>   O may we all remember well
>   The night of death draws near,"

sang the wife, in her sweet voice, sitting close to her husband's chair, so that he could hear the words.

Not long afterwards the Major said he was tired; it was not often that he was tired so early in the evening, but to-night, for some reason, he felt quite weary; he thought he would go to bed. It was half-past eight; at nine he and Scar were both asleep, and the two women left the house together. Walley's Cove was not far from the Farms, but it was farther up the mountain, where there was no road, only paths; they could not, therefore, go in the carriage; they could have taken Caleb Inches with them, but in that peaceful neighborhood escort for mere safety's sake was not necessary, and they preferred to be alone.

"Take my arm, mamma," said Sara, as they began to ascend.

But Madam Carroll would not. She walked on unaided. Her step was firm. She did not once speak.

In the small room under the roof, which he had occupied since his return, lay the young man who was now dying; for it needed but one glance to show that the summons had come: he was passing away. The farmer's wife, much affected, knelt beside him; the doctor had gone, she said, but a short time before; there was nothing more that he could do, and he was needed elsewhere. The farmer himself was fanning the unconscious face. Madam Carroll took the fan.

"Let me do that," she said. "I know you feel as if your children were needing you down-stairs."

For the three little children had been left alone in the room below, and, disturbed by the absence of father and mother, were not asleep; one of them had begun to cry a little at intervals. The farmer went down, his clumsy boots making no sound on the uncarpeted stairway, so careful was his tread. Madam Carroll sat down on the edge of the poor bed, and fanned the sleeping face; the eyes were closed, the long, dark lashes lay on the thin cheeks, the breath came slowly through the slightly parted lips. The farmer's wife began to pray in a low voice; she was a devout Baptist, and she had had her pastor there in the afternoon, and had fancied that the dying man was conscious for a time, and that he had listened and responded. She had grown fond of the poor

musician in taking care of him, and the tears rolled
down her sunburned cheeks as she prayed. Madam
Carroll remained calm; she moved the fan with even
sweep to and fro. She had taken off her bonnet, as
the night was warm, and with her golden curls, her
pink-tinted complexion, and the same pretty dress
she had worn to church in the morning, she was a
contrast to the rough, bare room, to the farmer's wife,
in her coarse homespun gown, and even to her own
daughter, who, in her plain black dress, her face pale
and sad, was standing near.

An hour passed. The child's wail below had now
in it the unmistakable sound of suffering. "Pray go
down," said Madam Carroll; "I am sure your baby
needs you."

"But I don't like to leave you, Madam Carroll;
it doesn't seem right," the woman answered, yet listening, too, at the same time, to the baby's wail
below.

"You need have no hesitation. I have had experience of this kind before; and besides, I do not
easily lose my self-possession."

"Yes, you *hev* got a strong hold on yersel," said
the farmer's wife admiringly. They spoke in low
tones, though sounds of earth could no longer penetrate to that gray, still border-land which the sleeper's
soul was crossing. "I know you keer for the poor

young man; you keer for him as much as I do. For
yer see he ain't got no mother to be sorry for him,
poor fellow," she continued, laying her rough hand
tenderly on his head; "and you and me knows,
Madam Carroll, how his mother'd feel. There ain't
nothing like the way a mother keers for her boy."

Sara came forward. "I am sure your child needs
you, Mrs. Walley," she said; "please go down at
once. I promise to call you if anything should be
needed."

The child was crying again, and the mother went.
Sara softly closed the door. It had not been closed
until then.

A little before midnight, Dupont, who had been
for six hours in a lethargic sleep, stirred and woke.
Madam Carroll bent over him. He knew her; he
turned his head towards her and lay looking at her,
his large eyes strangely solemn in their unmoving
gaze. Sara came and stood on the other side of the
bed, fanning him with the fan which her mother had
relinquished. Thus he remained, looking at Madam
Carroll, with his slow, partially comprehending stare.
Then gradually the stare grew conscious and intelligent. And then it grew full of expression. It was
wonderful to see the mind come back and look once
more from the windows of its deserted house of clay
—the last look on earth. Madam Carroll, bending

towards him, returned his gaze; she had laid one hand on his forehead, the other on his breast; her fair hair touched his shoulder. She said nothing; she did not move; but all her being was concentrated in her eyes. The dying man also was silent: probably he had passed beyond the power of speech. Thus, motionless, they continued to look at each other for a number of minutes. Then consciousness faded, the light left the windows; a few seconds more and the soul was gone. Madam Carroll, still in silence, laid her hand upon the heart and temples; all was still. Then she gently closed the eyes.

Sara, weeping, came to her side. "Do not, Sara; some one might come in," said her mother. Her hands rested on the closed lids. Then, her task done, she stood for a moment beside the couch, silently, looking at the still face on the pillow. "You must go down and tell them," she said, in a composed tone. "Farmer Walley must go immediately for Sabrina Barnes and her sister. You can say that the funeral will be from this house, and that they had better ask their own minister—the one who was here this afternoon—to officiate."

"Oh, mamma, do not try to think of everything; it is not necessary now," said Sara, beseechingly.

"Do as I tell you, Sara," answered Madam Carroll. And Sara obeyed her.

"THE LAST LOOK ON EARTH."

When she returned, Madam Carroll was arranging the pillows and straightening the coarse sheet. She had folded the musician's thin hands over his breast and smoothed his disordered hair.

"The child has been in pain all this time," said the daughter, "and they are frightened; Farmer Walley will go for Sabrina Barnes and for the doctor at the same time. I told Mrs. Walley that she need not come up, that we would stay. In any case she could hardly leave her baby now. But oh, mamma, do not try to do that; do not try to do anything more."

"Yes, we will stay," said Madam Carroll. She took a chair, placed it beside the bed, so that it faced the figure lying there, and sat down; she put her feet on a footstool and folded her hands.

"Dear mamma, do not sit there looking like that; do not try to be so quiet. No one will be here for half an hour: cry, mamma; let yourself cry. You have this little time, and—and it will be your last."

"I will not cry," answered Madam Carroll; "I have not cried at all; tears I can keep back. But I should like to kiss him, Sara, if you will keep watch. He would like to have his mother kiss him once before he goes away." And bending forward as she sat, she kissed tenderly the forehead and the closed eyes. The touch overcame her; she did not weep, but, putting her arms round him, she sat looking at him piteously. "He was such a dear little baby!" she murmured. "I was so proud of him! He was always so handsome and so brave—such a sturdy little fellow! When he was only six years old he said, 'I want to grow up quick and be big, so that I can take care of you, mamma.'" She stroked back his dark hair. "You meant no harm; none of it was your fault, Julian. Do not think your mother has any blame for you, my darling boy. But *now* you know that I have not." She passed her hands softly over his wasted cheeks. "May I put him in our—in your—lot in the church-yard, Sara? It will only take a little space, and the lot is so large; there isn't any other place where I should like to have him lying. People would think it was our kindness; in that way it could be done. And do not put me too far from him, when my time comes; not *too* far. For you know he was, Sara, my dear boy, my darling first-born son." She murmured this over and over, her arms round him. Then, "He is not lying quite straight," she said. And she tried to move his head a little. But already it had the strange heaviness of death, it was like a weight of stone in her small hands. As she realized this, her face became convulsed for the first time; her whole frame was shaken by her grief.

Footsteps were now audible coming up the mountain path outside. "Mamma, they are here," said Sara, from her post at the window.

But Madam Carroll had already controlled herself. She rose, pressed one long, last kiss on the still face; then she went to the door and opened it. When Sabrina Barnes and her sister, the two old women who in that rural neighborhood filled the office of watching by the dead, came up the stairs, she was waiting for them. In a clear, low voice she gave them her directions: the expenses of the funeral she should herself assume. Then she passed down the stairs with Sara on her way home, stopping to speak to the mother of the sick child in the lower room, and suggest some new remedy,

Mrs. Walley was distressed at the idea of their going home alone; but her husband had not yet returned, and the ladies did not wish to wait. The path was safe enough; it was only the loneliness of it. But the ladies said that they did not mind the loneliness. They went down the mountain by the light of the stars, reaching the Farms a little after two o'clock. Dupont had died at midnight.

The funeral took place on Tuesday afternoon. The Baptist minister officiated, but all the congregation of St. John's were also present. The farm-house was full, and people stood in the garden outside bare-

11

headed and reverent. Then the little procession was formed, and went down the mountain towards St. John's, where the Carrolls, with their usual goodness, as everybody said, had given a place for the poor stranger in their own lot. The coffin was borne on men's shoulders in the old-fashioned way. It was covered with flowers. Every one had sent some, for they all remembered how fond he had been of their flower-gardens. They recalled his sweet voice and his songs, his merry ways with children. There was a pathos, too, in his poverty, because they had not suspected it. And so they all thought of him kindly as he was borne by on his way to his last rest.

Madam Carroll and Sara had not been at the farm-house. But they were at the grave. They were in waiting there when the procession entered the church-yard gate. They stood at the head of the coffin as it rested on the bier during the prayer. They stood there while it was lowered, and while the grave was being filled. This was the custom in Far Edgerley: everybody stayed. But when this task was completed the people dispersed; the services were considered at an end.

Flower had begun to shape the mound, and Madam Carroll still waited. Seeing this, several persons came back, and a little group gathered.

"Ah, well, poor friendless young man, his life here

is over," said Mrs. Greer. "It is not quite straight, Flower; if you come here and look, you can see for yourself."

"I suppose he was a foreigner," said Miss Sophy; "he looked like one. Didn't you say that you thought he was a foreigner, Madam Carroll?"

"He came from Martinique," answered the Major's wife; "he had lived there, I believe, or on one of the neighboring islands, almost all his life."

"Well, I call that foreign; I call all the West India Islands very foreign," said Miss Sophy. "They don't seem to me civilized. They are principally inhabited by blacks."

"It was so sad that he had no money," remarked Mrs. Rendlesham. "We never dreamed of that, you know. Though I remember now that his clothes, when you came to really look at them, were a little —a little worn, perhaps."

"They were shabby," said Miss Corinna, not with unkindness, but simply as historian.

"Is it true, Madam Carroll, that he was a Baptist?" asked Miss Bolt, thoughtfully looking at the mound.

"The Walleys are Baptists, you know," answered the lady of the Farms. "They had their pastor there several times, and on the last day Mrs. Walley was sure that Mr.—Mr. Dupont was conscious, and that he joined in their prayers, and assented to what was said."

"I don't believe he was *anything*—I mean, anything in particular," said Mrs. General Hibbard, decisively. "He hadn't that air."

"Oh, dear Mrs. Hibbard, surely we should be charitable," said little Miss Tappen, who was waiting with a wreath of her best chrysanthemums to place upon the completed mound.

"Well, Amelia, can you say he *had?*" said the General's widow, in an argumentative tone, with her forefinger extended.

"I suppose he had neither father nor mother, nor any near relatives, poor fellow, as he never spoke of them," observed Miss Dalley; "that is, I never heard that he did. But perhaps he talked more freely to you, Madam Carroll. Did he ever mention his parents?"

"Mamma, I think we had better go now," interposed Sara Carroll. "You are very tired, I know."

"Oh, yes," said all the ladies, "do go, dear Madam Carroll." "You have had so much to do lately." "You are looking quite fatigued, really." "Pray take care of yourself, for all our sakes."

Madam Carroll looked at the mound, which was now nearly completed. Then she made a little gesture of farewell to the group, and turned with her daughter towards the gate. All the ladies wore black dresses: it was the custom at Far Edgerley to

wear black at funerals. Madam Carroll not only
wore a black dress, but she had put a black ribbon
on her little straw bonnet.

"Isn't it sweet of her to do that?" said Miss Dalley. "It makes it a sort of mourning, you know;
and I like to think that the poor lonely fellow had
at least one mourner to stand beside his grave."

The path took the two ladies past the study. Its
door was open; the rector saw them, and came out.
He offered his arm in silence to Madam Carroll.
She took it. She was trembling a little. "I am
excessively tired," she said, as if apologizing.

"Yes, I noticed it during the prayer."

"Then you were there?" She spoke mechanically,
more as if she were filling the time that must pass
before they could reach the gate than as though she
cared for reply.

"I was both at the house and the grave," answered
Owen. He did not look at Sara, who was on the
other side of Madam Carroll. He could not. During all these days and nights of Dupont's last illness,
and since his death, he had been haunted by the
thought of the grief she must be enduring. And
yet to have seen the least trace of that grief in her
face (and he should be sure to see it, though others
might not), would have been intolerable to him. He
did not, therefore, once look at her; he was a man

of stern self-control as regarded his actions. But he could not help his feelings; and these gave him new suffering as he walked on, so near her, yet separated from her by the gulf of that bitter knowledge. Their carriage was waiting at the gate; he assisted them in, bowed, and they drove away.

Scar and the Major were sitting at the open window of the library as the two ladies alighted at the door. "Mamma, it seems a *very* long time since you and sister Sara went away," said the child, leaning out to speak to them. " Papa and I have taken a walk, and looked at all our pictures, and told all our stories; and now we are sitting here waiting for you."

"I will come in a few minutes, my pet," said Madam Carroll.

Sara went directly to the library, and sat down beside her father's chair. He wished to hear all about the funeral of "that poor young man," and she answered his questions at length, and told him everything she could think of in connection with it. The Major had known Dupont but vaguely; he had seen him at the reception, but the face had faded from his memory, and he should not have known him had they met again. He was a musical genius who had appeared among them. He was glad that he had appeared; it was a variety, and they had so little variety in Far Edgerley. Good music was always an addition, and Marion was very fond of music, very; he was glad she could have this little enjoyment. He had said this to Marion several times. But it was a sad end—very—to die alone among strangers, so far from home.

After some delay, Madam Carroll came in. She had taken off her black dress and put on a bright little gown of blue; her hair had been recurled, and there was a lovely color in her cheeks, and some sprays of cream-colored honeysuckle in her blue belt. As she came nearer, the Major's old eyes dwelt upon her with childlike pleasure and pride. "You are looking very charming this evening, Madam Carroll," he said, with his old-fashioned gallantry.

She sat down beside him. "Sara has been telling me about the funeral of that unfortunate young musician," he continued. "It was like you, Marion, to show so much kindness to the poor fellow, whoever he was, and I am glad you did it. Kindness to the unfortunate and the stranger has always been an especial characteristic of the Carroll family, and you have merely represented me in this matter, done what I, of course, should have done had I been well —had I quite recovered from my illness of last winter, you know. But I am much improved—much improved. This poor young man seems to have been utterly alone in the world, since even when he was dying, and knew that he was, he told no one, as I understand it, anything of his parentage, or life, or history, and left no letters or even a message for friends. It is really quite remarkable."

"Papa," said Sara, "now that we are all here, wouldn't it be a good time to look at the new photographs?" The photographs were views of English scenery which she had sent for; the Major had been in England, and liked to relate reminiscences of his visit. He was interested at once.

"Certainly," he answered, with alacrity, "an excellent idea. Scar, get the boxes."

Scar brought the boxes, and gave one of them to his mother; as he did so his hand touched hers. "Why, mamma, are you so cold?" he said, in surprise. "It is still summer, mamma, and quite warm."

"It is nothing," answered Madam Carroll; "only a passing chill. It is over now."

CHAPTER VII.

A few days after the funeral of the musician the Major was taken ill. It was not the failure of strength, which often came over him, nor the confused feeling in the head, of which he never spoke, but which his wife always recognized when she saw him sitting with his forehead bent and his hand over his eyes. This time he had fever, and was slightly delirious; he seemed also to be in pain. Madam Carroll and Sara did not leave him; they were in deep anxiety. But in the evening relief came; the fever ceased, and he fell into a quiet sleep. The two women kissed him softly, and, still anxious, stole into the next room to keep the watch, leaving the door open between the two. A shaded night-lamp faintly illumined the room where he lay, but the outer one was in darkness. Scar had gone to bed, and the house was very still; they could hear the murmur of the brook through the open window; for although it was now towards the last of October, it was still summer in that favored land. The outer room was

large, and they sat on a sofa at its far end; they
could talk in low tones without danger of disturbing
the Major, whose sleeping face they could see through
the open door.

The moon rose. Madam Carroll went into the
Major's room and closed the dark curtains, so that
the increasing light should not waken him; when
she came back the silver radiance had reached Sara,
and was illuminating her face and figure as she leaned
against the cushions of the sofa. "He is sleeping
naturally and restfully now," said the wife, as she
took her seat again; "his face has lost that look of
pain it has had all day. But do you know that you
yourself are looking far from well, Sara?"

"I know it. And I am ashamed of it. When I
see you doing everything, and bearing everything,
without one outward sign, without the least change
in your face or expression, I am ashamed that I have
so little self-control."

"Have you been supposing, then, that all this un-
varying pink and white color was my own? Have
you never suspected that I put it on?—that it was
fictitious? I began in July—you know when. It
was for that reason that I altered the hours of our
receptions from afternoon to evening: candle-light
is more favorable, you know. I also began then to
wear a little lace veil. You think me about thirty-

five, don't you? I am forty-eight. I was thirty-five when I married the Major. All this golden hair would be heavily streaked with gray if I should let it alone."

"Do not feel obliged to tell me anything, mamma."

"I prefer that you should know; and it is also a relief to me to tell," answered Madam Carroll, her eyes on the dark outline of the mountains, visible in the moonlight through the open window. "My poor little Cecilia passed easily for six, she was so small and frail, like Scar; in reality she was over ten. The story was, you know, that I had been married the first time at sixteen. That part was true; but nineteen years had passed instead of seven, as they supposed. You are wondering, probably, why I should have deceived your father in such little things, matters unimportant. There had been no plan for deceiving him; it had been begun before I met him; he simply believed what the others believed. And later I found that they were not unimportant to him—those little things; they were important. He thought a great deal of them. He thought a great deal of my youth; youth and ignorance of the world, child-like inexperience, had made up his ideal of me, and by the time I found it out, his love and goodness, his dear protection, had become so much to me that I could not run the risk of

losing them by telling him his mistake. I know now
that I need not have feared this, I need not have
feared anything where he was concerned; but I did
not know then, and I was afraid. He saw in me a
little blue-eyed, golden-haired girl-mother, unacquainted with the dark side of life, trusting, sweet.
It was this very youth and childlike look which had
attracted him, man of the world as he was himself,
and no longer young. I feared to shatter his dream.
In addition, that part did not seem to me of any
especial consequence; I knew that I should be able
to live up to his ideal, to maintain it not only fully,
but longer, probably, than as though I had been in
reality the person he supposed me to be; for now it
would be a purpose, determinedly and carefully carried out, and not mere chance. I knew that I could
look the same for years longer; I have that kind of
diminutive prettiness which, with attention, does not
change; and I should give the greatest attention. I
felt, too, that I should always be entirely devoted to
him. Gallant and handsome as he was, he was not
young, and I knew that I should care for him just
the same through illness, age, or infirmity; for I have
that kind of faithfulness (many women haven't) and
—I loved him.

"And as to my little dead boy, there again there
had been no plan for deceiving him. People had

supposed from my young face that I could have been married but a year or two, and that Cecilia had been my only child. It was imagined from my silence that my marriage had not been a happy one—they said I had that look—and therefore no one questioned me; they took it all for granted. I said that my husband was dead. But I said no more. I had decided, for Cecilia's sake, to keep the secret of the manner of his death: why should her innocent life be clouded by the story of her father? Besides, could I go about proclaiming, relating, his—shortcomings? He was my husband, though he had cared so little for me; he was my husband, though he had taken from me my darling little son. And about that son, my poor little drowned boy, I simply had never been able to speak; the hurt was too deep; I could not have spoken without telling what I had decided not to tell, for where he was concerned I could not have invented. Thus I had kept the secret at first from loyalty to my dead husband, and for the sake of my little girl; I kept it later, Sara, because I was afraid. The Major loved me—yes; but would he continue to love me if he should know that instead of being the youthful little woman barely twenty-three, I was over thirty-five? that instead of being inexperienced, unacquainted with the dark side of life, I knew all, had been through all? that instead

of the dear little girl's being my only child, I was the
mother of a son who, had he lived, would have been
a man almost full-grown—would he continue to love
me through all this? I was afraid he would not.

" Remember that *I* had not planned his idea of me,
I had had nothing to do with it; he had made it himself. Remember, too, that such as it was, I knew I
could live up to it, that he need never be disappointed, that I could fully realize his dream. In
that, at least, I have succeeded. I have lived up to
it, I have *been* it, so long, that there have even been
times when I have seemed to myself to really be the
pretty, bright little wife, thirty years younger than
her husband, that I was pretending to be. But that
feeling can never come again.

" I am not excusing myself to you, Sara, in all
this; I am only explaining myself. Under the
same circumstances you would never have done it,
nor under twenty times the same circumstances.
But I am not you; I am not anybody but myself.
That lofty kind of vision which sees only the one
path, and that the highest, is not mine; I always
see all the shorter paths, lower down, that lead to
the same place—the cross-cuts. I can do little things
well, and I can do a great many of them; I have
that kind of small and ever-present cleverness. But
the great things, the wide view—they are beyond

me. And do not forget, too, how much it was to
me. It was everything. I was alone in the world
with my delicate little girl, who needed so much
that I could not give—luxuries, constant care, the
best advice. I had strained every nerve, made use
of all my poor little knowledge and my trifling ac-
complishments; I had worked as hard as I possibly
could; and the result of all my efforts was that I
had barely succeeded in getting our bread from day
to day, with nothing laid up for the future, and the
end of my small strength near at hand. For I was
not fitted for that kind of struggle, and I knew that
I was not. I could work and plan and accomplish,
and even, I believed, successfully, but only when
sheltered—sheltered in a home, no matter how plain,
protected from actual contact with the crowd. In a
crowd there is always brutality; in a crowd I lost
heart. What were my small plans, which always
concerned themselves with the delicate little things
and details, in the great pushing struggle for bread?
It was when I was fully realizing the hopelessness
of all my efforts, when the future was at its black-
est, and I could not look at Cecilia without danger
of tears—for they had told me that something might
be done for her during the next year—for her poor
spine—and I had not the money to pay for it—it was
then that your father's love came to me like a gift

straight down from heaven. But do not think that
I did not love him in return—really love him for
himself, not for what he gave me. I did. I do. I
had suffered so much, my life had been so crushed
under sorrow and trouble, that, save my love for
Cecilia, I seemed to myself to have no feelings left;
I thought they were all dead. But when the Major
began to love me, when he spoke—oh, then I knew
that they were not! I felt that I had never known
what real happiness was until that day; and my
whole heart turned to him. There was gratitude
in my love, I do not deny it; but the gratitude was
for my little girl—the love was all for him. It has
never lessened, Sara, from that hour.

" It seemed to me such a wonderful thing that he
should love me! It gave me such a strange surprise
that he should care for my little doll-like face and
curls. But when I found that he did care for them,
how precious they became to me, how hard I tried
to keep them pretty for his sake! And, for his sake,
I not only kept them pretty, but I made them prettier. I was a far prettier woman after the Major
married me than I was before; I had a motive to
be so. Ah, yes, I loved him, Sara! May you never
have a comprehension of the ill-usage, the suffering,
I had been through! but still, without such knowledge, you will hardly be able to understand the depth

of my love for him. When he first saw me, I was making an effort to seem comparatively cheerful; I was spending a few weeks with Mrs. Upton, the wife of an army officer, at Mayberry, and I did not want her to suspect my inward despair. Mrs. Upton had known me at Natchez while I was trying to keep a little school there, and when I came to Mayberry to try again, she asked me to come and spend a few weeks with her before I began. She knew that I was poor—she did not know how poor—and she had always been fond of Cecilia, who was—surely I may say it now—a very beautiful child. Think of it all, Sara; remember the needs of the child; remember what he was himself, and—that I loved him."

"I do think of it. And I do not blame you," Sara Carroll answered, speaking not as the daughter, but as one woman speaks to another. "You have made my father's life a very happy one."

"I have tried; but it has always been in my own narrow way, the little things of each day and hour. It was the only way I knew."

There was a silence; the room had grown dark, as a broad bank of cloud came slowly over the moon.

"Cecilia is with her brother to-night," said Madam Carroll, after a while; "Cecilia is a woman now, a woman in heaven. She was twenty-two on the 11th of September. I wonder what they are saying to

12

each other! He used to be so fond of her, so proud when I let him hold her for a few minutes in his strong little arms! They will be sure to meet and talk together; don't you think so?"

"How can we know, mamma?" said Sara, sadly.

"We cannot. Yet we do," answered Madam Carroll. "I know it; I am sure of it." She was silent for a moment; then went on speaking softly in the darkness, as if half to herself. "His poor clothes, Sara—oh, so neglected and worn!—I could not bear it when I saw them. I had asked him about them more than once, and he always said that they were in good order—that is, good enough. But I pressed him; I wanted to see with my own eyes; and at last I succeeded in persuading him to bring a few of them late in the evening when no one would see him, and put them under the hedge near the gate; then, when everybody was asleep, I stole down to get them, took them into the sitting-room, lighted the lamp, and looked at them. In 'good order' he had called them, poor boy, when they were almost rags. I cried over those clothes, Sara ; I could not help it; they were the only tears I shed. It showed so plainly what his life had been. I could not help remembering in what careful order were all his little frocks and jackets when he was my dear little child. After that I made him bring me a few things once

a week. I gave him a little old carpet-bag of mine
to put them in. I used to mend them in my dress-
ing-room, with the door locked, whenever I had a
little leisure (I took only my leisure), and then I carried them down and put them under the hedge when
I knew he was coming. It was a comfort to me to
do it; but he didn't care anything about the mend-
ing himself—he said so. He had lived so long with
his poor things neglected and ragged that he didn't
know any other way. Yet he tried, too, after his
fashion—a man's fashion—to dress well. Don't you
remember his red silk handkerchiefs and socks, and
his silk-lined umbrella? Poor boy, he had the wish;
but not the money or the knowledge. How could
he learn, living where and as he had? That watch-
chain and ring he had when he came back—they
were only gilt."

The grieving story was no longer uttered aloud,
the low tones ceased. But the mother was pursuing
the train of thought in her own mind.

After a while she spoke again. "I was so unwilling to tell you, Sara, to burden you with it all!
Nothing could have made me do it but the fear of
—of that which afterwards *did* happen—death. For
when he came back after that illness, and I saw how
changed he was, how weak, and knew that I had
nothing to help him with, then I felt desperate. I

knew that he ought to return to that warmer climate, and at once; I had nothing of my own, and
the Major's money, of course, I would not take.
Yours is not his, and so I came to you; I knew that
you would help me to the utmost of your power—
as you have. But if there had been any possible
alternative, anything else in the world that I could
have done—and I thought over everything—I want
you to believe that I should never have come to you."

"It was too much for you to bear alone, mamma."

"No, it was not that; I could have borne much
more. I have borne it. But what I could not bear
was that he should be ill. I had exhausted every
means I had when he went away the first time;
there was nothing left. I had given all I had—all,
excepting things which the Major himself had given
me. I had even stretched a point, and added the
watch your uncle Mr. Chase sent me when I was
married. There was the little breast-pin, also, that
Mrs. Upton gave me at the same time. Then
there was the gold thimble and the sleeve-buttons
you sent me from Longfields, and the gold pencil
Senator Ashley gave me one Christmas. I even put
in my little coral necklace. It had belonged to Cecilia, and was the only thing I had left from her
baby days; it was of little, almost no value intrin-
sically, as I knew, because I had tried to sell it more

than once when she and I were so poor; but if it could add even a few shillings to the hoard — so small! — that was to take him back to the climate he needed, I was glad to have it go. I tell you this only to show you that absolute necessity, and that alone, drove me to you."

"I am so glad you came, mamma!—glad that I was able to help you, or at least that you let me try."

"Yes, you were glad to help me; you were very kind and good," answered the Major's wife. Then, sitting erect, and with a quicker utterance, "But you were always afraid of him. You never trusted him. You were always afraid that he would be traitorous, that he would go to your father. *I* was never afraid; I knew that he would never betray; he cared too much for me, for his poor mother; for although he had not been with me since he was a child, in his way he loved me. He was never selfish, he was only unthinking, my poor, neglected boy! But *you* never gave him any mercy; you suspected him to the last."

"Oh, no, mamma; I tried—"

"Yes, you tried. But you were always Miss Carroll, always scornful at heart, cold. You endured him; that was all. And do not think he did not see it, was not hurt by it! But I did not mean to

reproach you, Sara; it is not just. I will stop this
minute." She brought one hand down into the
palm of the other with a decided little sound, and
held them thus pressed tightly together for several
minutes. Then, letting them fall apart, she leaned
her head back against the cushions again. "You
were thinking of your father," she said, in a gentler
tone; "that was the cause of all, of your coldness,
your fear. You were afraid that Julian would do
something to distress him, to disturb his peace. But
he would never have done that. You did not know
him, Sara; you never in the least comprehended
him. But I must not keep going back to that.
Rather tell me—and speak truthfully, it can make
no difference now—do you think there was any
time, after my poor boy's first coming, when we
could have safely told the Major?"

"No," answered the Major's daughter, "there was
no time. He could not have borne it; the surprise,
the shock, would have been too great."

"So it seemed to me. But I wanted your opinion too. You see, about me there is more than there
used to be in his mind, or, rather, in his fancy: he
doesn't distinguish. What were once surmises he
now thinks facts, and he fully believes in them. He
has constructed a sort of history, and has woven in
all sorts of imaginary theories in the most curious

way. For instance, he thinks that my mother was one of a family well known in New York—so they tell me, at least; I know little of New York—the Forsters of Forster's Island. My mother was plain Mary Foster, from Chester, Vermont, or its neighborhood, a farmer's daughter. In the same way he has built up a belief that my father was an Episcopal clergyman, and that he was educated in England. My father was a Baptist missionary; he was a man of fair education (he educated me), but he was never in England in his life. These are only parts of it, his late fancies about me. To have brushed them all away, to have told him that they were false, that I had all along been deceiving him, to have bewildered him, given him so much pain—my dear gray-haired old Major! Oh, Sara, I could never have done it! 'A son?' he would have said, perplexed. 'But there is only little Scar.' It would have been cruelty, he believes in me so!" Her voice quivered, and she stopped.

"He has never had more cause to believe in you than now, mamma—to believe in your love for him; he does not know it, but some day he will. You have been so unswerving in your determination to make secure, first of all, his happiness and tranquillity, so unmindful of your own pain, that it seems to me, his daughter, as if you had never been so faithful a wife to him as now."

" Oh, say it again !" said Madam Carroll, burying her face in her hands. " I did my best, or at least I tried; but I have been so—tortured—harassed—"

The Major stirred in the next room; they hurried softly in. He was awake; he turned his head and looked at his wife as she stood beside the bed. " You and Sara both here ?" he said. " Did I go to bed, then, very early this evening ?" He did not wait for reply, but went on. " I have had such a beautiful dream, Marion; it was about that drive we took when we were first married—do you remember ? Through the woods near Mayberry. There was that same little stream that we had to cross so many times, and the same bank where you got out and gathered wild violets, and the same spring where we drank, and that broken bridge where you were so frightened—do you remember ?"

" Yes," answered his wife, brightly; " and I remember, too, that you lost your way, and pretended that you had not, and wouldn't ask, for fear I should suspect it."

The Major laughed, feebly, but with enjoyment. "I didn't want *you* to know that *I* didn't know everything—even the country roads," he answered. " For I was old enough to be your father, and you were such a little thing; I had my dignity to keep up, you see." He laughed again. " That spring was

very cold, wasn't it?" he said, and he lay thinking
of it for a minute or two. Then slowly his eyes
closed; he had fallen asleep. They waited, but he
did not waken. His sleep was peaceful, and they
went back again to their watch in the outer room.

"It is two o'clock, mamma. Won't you lie down
for a while? I am strong, and not at all tired; if
he should waken, I will at once call you."

"I could not sleep," answered Madam Carroll,
taking her former seat. "We could neither of us
sleep, I fancy, while there was the least danger of
the fever's returning—as the doctor said it might."

"I thought perhaps you might rest, even if you
did not sleep."

"I shall never be any more rested than I am
now," answered the Major's wife. After a silence
of some length she spoke again; "In all this we
should not forget Mr. Owen," she said, as though
taking up a task which must be performed. "I feel
sure that he is suffering deeply. You know what
he must be thinking?"

"So long as he does not speak, what he thinks is
of small consequence," said Miss Carroll.

"It may be so to you. It is not to him." She
paused. "I can remember that I once liked him,"
she went on, in a monotonous tone. "And I can
even believe that I shall like him again. But not

now, not now.   Now it is too near—those cruel
words he spoke about my boy."

"He did not know—"

"Of course he did not; and I try to be just.   He
was angry, hurt, alarmed; he was hurt that I should
treat him as I did—I treated him horribly—and he
was alarmed about you.   I have never thanked you
for what you did that day, Sara—the day he came
to warn us; I could not.   For I knew how you
loathed it—the expedient you took.   You only took
it because there was no other."

"You are very hard to me, mamma."

"About your feeling I am; how can I help it?
But not about the deed: that was noble.   In order
to help me you let Mr. Owen suppose that you were
engaged to a man he—he utterly despised.   Well,
you helped me.   But you hurt him; you hurt
Frederick Owen that morning about as deeply as
you could."   She moved to Sara's side in the darkness, took her hand with a quick grasp and held it
in both her own.   "And you are so proud," she
whispered softly, "that you will never acknowledge
that you hurt yourself too; that the sacrifice you
then made in lowering yourself by your own act in
his eyes was as great a one as a woman can make;
for he loves you devotedly, jealously, and you—*you*
know how much you care for him."

Without leaving time for reply, she moved back to her former place, and went on with what she had been saying, as though that sudden soft interpolated whisper had not existed. " Yes—this strange double feeling that I have about Frederick Owen makes me even feel sorry for him at times, sorry to have him suffer as I know he must be suffering, sorry to have him think what I know he must be thinking of you ; and also of me. For he thinks that you had a liking for a man whom he considered unworthy to speak your name (oh, detestable arrogance !); he thinks that it was clandestine, that you dared not tell your father ; and that I was protecting you in it as well as I could ; all this, of course, he must believe. Death has put an end to it, and now it will never be known ; this also he is thinking. But, meanwhile, *he* knows it. And he cannot forget it. He thinks you have in your heart the same feeling still. But I remembered—I did what I could for you by telling him that it was but a fancy of the moment, that it would pass."

" Oh !" murmured Sara, with a quick, involuntary gesture of repulsion ; then she stopped.

" I was trying to pave a way out of it for you. You do not like the way, because it includes — includes the supposition that you-- But one can never please you, Sara Carroll !"

She rose and began to walk swiftly to and fro across the room, her footsteps making no sound on the thick, faded, old-fashioned carpet—a relic from the days of the Sea Island Carrolls.

"What do you want me to do?" she said, abruptly, as she passed Sara for the fourth time.

"If you are alluding to Mr. Owen, I don't want you to do anything," answered Miss Carroll.

"Oh, you are proud! For the present nothing can be done. But let me tell you one thing—do not be *too* repellent. 'Tis good in me to warn you, to take his part, when I hate him so—hate him for what he said. Do you suppose I would have had him reading prayers over my poor dead boy after what had passed? Never in the world. No one who despised him should come near him. So I had the Baptist minister. I was a Baptist myself when I was a girl—if I ever was a girl! All this hurts *you*, of course; but I cannot help it. Be patient. Some day I shall forgive him. Perhaps soon." She had paused in front of Sara as she said this, for they had both been guardedly careful to speak in the lowest tones.

The girl left her place on the sofa; she rose and walked beside her stepmother as she resumed her quick, restless journey to and fro across the floor. They came and went in silence for many minutes.

Then Sara put her arm round Madam Carroll, and drew her towards the sofa again.

"Rest awhile, mamma," she said, placing the cushions so that she could lie easily; "you do not know how very tired you are." And Madam Carroll for a half-hour yielded.

"We must bear with each other, Sara," she said, as she lay with her eyes closed. "For amid all our other feelings, there is one which we have in common, our love for your father. That is and always must be a tie between you and me."

"Always," answered Sara.

A little after daylight the Major woke. There had been no return of the fever; he had slept in peace while they kept the vigil near him; his illness was over. As he opened his eyes, his wife came to the bedside; she had just risen—or so it seemed, for she wore a rose-colored wrapper, and on her head a little lace cap adorned with rose-colored ribbon. The Major had not seen the cap before; he thought it very pretty.

"Trying to be old, are you, Madam Carroll?" he said; "old and matronly?"

Sara came in not long afterwards; she, too, was freshly dressed in a white wrapper.

"I have brought you your breakfast, papa," she said.

"Isn't it earlier than usual?" asked the Major, turning his dim eyes towards the window. But he could not see the light of the sunrise on the peaks.

"I am afraid, Major, that you are growing indolent," said Madam Carroll, with pretended severity, as she poured out his tea.

"Indolent?" said the Major—"indolent? Indolence is nothing to vanity. And you and Sara, in your pink and white gowns, are living images of vanity this morning, Madam Carroll."

"I AM AFRAID, MAJOR, THAT YOU ARE GROWING INDOLENT."

CHAPTER VIII.

AUTUMN at last came over the mountains; she decked them in her most sumptuous colors, and passed slowly on towards the south. The winds followed the goddess, eight of them; they came sounding their long trumpets through the defiles; they held carnival in the high green valleys; they attacked the forests and routed the lighter foliage, but could not do much against the stiff, dark ranks of the firs. They careered over all the peaks; sometimes they joined hands on Chillawassee's head, and whirled round in a great circle, laughing loudly, for half a day; and then the little people who lived on the ground said to each other that it " blew from all round the sky."

They came to Far Edgerley more than once; they blew through Edgerley Street; at night the villagers in their beds heard the long trumpets through the near gorges, and felt their houses shake. But they were accustomed to these autumn visitors; they had a theory, too, that this great sweeping of their peaks

13

and sky was excellent for their mountain air. And upon the subject of their air there was much conceit in Far Edgerley.

When at length the winds had betaken themselves to the lowlands, with the intention of blowing across the levels of Georgia and Florida, and coming round to surprise the northerners at Indian River and St. Augustine, the quiet winter opened in the mountains they had left behind them. The Major had had no return of his October illness; he came to church on Sundays as usual, and appeared at his wife's receptions. It was noticed, although no one spoke of it, that he did not hold himself quite so erect as formerly, and that perhaps his eyesight was not quite so good; but he still remained to his village the exemplar of all that was noble and distinguished, and they admired him and talked about him as much as ever. He was their legend, their escutcheon; so long as they had him they felt distinguished themselves.

The winter amusements began about Christmas-time. They consisted principally of the Sewing Society and the Musical Afternoons. To these entertainments "the gentlemen" came in the evening —F. Kenneway, Mr. Phipps, the junior warden, and the rector, when they could get him. A Whist Club had, indeed, been proposed. There was a double motive in this proposal. There were persons in the congregation who considered whist-playing a test of the best churchmanship; these were secretly desirous to see the test applied to the new rector, or rather the new rector applied to it. But the thoughtful Mrs. Greer, having foreseen this very possibility at an early date in the summer, had herself sounded the rector upon the subject, and brought back a negative upon the end of her delicate conversational line. She had asked him if he thought that the sociability engendered by card-tables at small parties could, in his opinion, counterbalance the danger which familiarity with the pasteboard squares might bring to their young men (Phipps and Kenneway); and whether he himself, at moments of leisure, and when he wished to rest from intellectual fatigue, of which, of course, he must have *so* much, ever whiled away the time with these same gilded symbols, not with others, but by himself.

Owen, who had not for the moment paid that attention to the eloquence of Mrs. Greer which he should have done, did not understand her. He had received an impression of cymbals. This was no surprise to him; he had found Mrs. Greer capable of the widest range of subjects.

"I mean the painted emblems, you know—cards," explained Mrs. Greer; "clubs, diamonds, and spades,

Mr. Owen. Nor should we leave out hearts. I was referring, when I spoke, to solitaire. But there is also whist. Whist is, in its way, a climate by itself —a climate of geniality."

This was a phrase of Madam Carroll's. Mrs. Greer had collected a large assortment of phrases from the overflow of the Farms. These she treasured, and dealt out one by one; her conversation was richly adorned with them. She had excellent opportunities for collecting, as Madam Carroll had long been in the habit of telling her any little item which she wished to have put in circulation through the village in a certain guise. She always knew that her exact phrase would be repeated, but not as hers; it would be repeated as if it were original with the lady who spoke it. This was precisely what Madam Carroll intended. To have said herself, for instance, that the new chintz curtains of her drawing-room combined delicacy and durability, and a bower-like brightness, was too apparent; but for Mrs. Greer to say it (in every house on Edgerley Street) was perfectly proper, and accomplished the same result. The whole town remarked upon the delicacy and the durability and the bower-like brightness; and the curtains, which she had made and put up herself at small expense, took their place among the many other peculiarly admirable things possessed by the Farms.

Upon the present occasion, however, Mrs. Greer gave Madam Carroll's name to the phrase she had repeated; she thought it would have more influence. " Yes, that is what our dear Madam Carroll used to call it —a climate of geniality," she said, looking at the rector with an inquiring smile.

But, ignoring the phrase of the Farms, none the less did Owen bring out his negative; with the gilded symbols he did not amuse himself, either alone or in company.

Armed, therefore, with this knowledge, Mrs. Greer was ready; she met the project of the Whist Club in its bud, and vanquished it with a Literary Society, whose first four meetings she gave herself, with a delicate little hot supper thrown in. The Whist Club could not stand against this, Miss Honoria Ashley, who was its chief supporter, offering only apples and conversation. But a large cold apple on a winter night is not calculated to rouse enthusiasm; while, as to conversation, everybody knew that hot coffee promoted it. So the Literary Society conquered, and the whist test was not, for that season at least, applied to the churchmanship of the rector.

During these winter months Owen kept himself constantly busy. It was thought that he worked too hard. He looked tired; sometimes, young and strong as he was, he looked worn. There was a good deal of motherly anxiety about this; some sisterly, too. Ferdinand Kenneway said that he felt towards him like a brother. But Owen pursued his own course, unmindful of these sympathetic feelings. He came to Madam Carroll's receptions as usual, but did not stay long: he was the last to come and the first to go. He called at the Farms, though not often; and when he went there, he did not go alone.

So the winter passed on and departed, and spring came. Then a sorrow fell upon the little mountain town. Early one soft morning in March, when the cinnamon-colored tassels were out on the trees, and the air was warm and gray, with the smell of rain in it, word came down Edgerley Street, passing from house to house, that Carroll Farms had been visited in the night: the Major, their Major, had wakened quiet and content, but like a little child; the powers of his mind had been taken from him.

Every one had loved him, and now there was real mourning. They all said to each other and to themselves that they should never look upon his like again. The poor nation had greatly retrograded since his day; even their state was not what it had been; under these circumstances it could not be expected that the world should soon produce another Scarborough Carroll. They went over all the history of his life: his generous sharing of his fortune

with his half-brother; his silence under the forget-
fulness of that half-brother's children; his high position and many friends in the old army; his brilliant
record in the later army, their own army, vanquished,
but still dear to them, the army of the South; they
told again the story of his gallant ride round the
enemy's forces in the Valley, of his charge up the
hill at Fredericksburg, his last brave defence of the
bridge on the way to Appomattox. His wounds
were recalled, his shattered arm, the loss of his
money, so uncomplainingly borne; they spoke of his
beautiful courtesy to every one, and of his unfailing
kindness to all the poor. And then, how handsome
he was, how noble in bearing and expression, how
polished in manner! such a devoted husband and
father, so pure a patriot! Their dear old Major:
they could not say enough.

The junior warden kept his room all day; he could
not bear to hear it talked about. Then the next
morning out he went at an early hour to see everybody he knew, and he told them all how very impru-
dent Carroll had always been, recklessly so, recklessly. He was up and down Edgerley Street all day,
swinging his cane more than usual as he walked,
thus giving a light and juvenile air to his arms and
shoulders, which was perhaps somewhat contradicted
by the uncertain tread of his little old feet. In the

afternoon Frederick Owen went to the Farms; for
the first time since the preceding October he went
alone. Miss Carroll was in the drawing-room when
he came in; she was receiving a visit of general in-
quiry and condolence from the three Miss Rendleshams. They went away after a while, and then,
before he had had time to speak—as he stood there
realizing that he had not been alone with her since
that day, now six months in the past, when she had
told him of her engagement to Dupont—he saw
through the open door of the drawing-room the small
figure of Madam Carroll. She had not come down
to see the three Miss Rendleshams. But she did
come down to see the rector. She came straight to
him, with her quick, light step. "I heard that you
were here, and came down. I am anxious to see you,
Mr. Owen. Not to-day, but soon. I thought I
would come down myself and ask you; I did not
want to write a note."

"At any time you will name," answered Owen.
He had risen as she entered. Miss Carroll had
seemed to him unchanged, save that her eyes showed
that she had been crying; but the Major's wife, he
said to himself, with almost awe-struck astonish-
ment—the Major's wife, had he met her elsewhere,
he should hardly have known. Her veil of golden
hair, no longer curled, was put plainly back, and

fastened in a close knot behind; her eyes, the blue eyes he had always thought so pretty, looked tired and sunken and dim, with crows'-feet at their corners; all her lovely bloom was gone, and the whole of her little faded face was a net-work of minute wrinkles. She was still small and slender, and she still had her pretty features; but this was an old woman who was talking to him, and Madam Carroll had been so young.

"It will not be for some days yet, I think," she was saying. "I shall wait until the doctor has made up his mind. He wants more time, though I want none; when he does make it up, it will be as mine is now. But I prefer to wait until he sees clearly; will you ask him from day to day what he thinks, and, when he has decided, then will you come?"

"Yes," replied Owen. "But do you mean that the Major—"

"I mean that the Major is in no immediate danger; that he will continue about the same. He will not grow better, but neither will he grow much worse. He may be brighter at times, but he will not regain his memory; that is gone. But we shall not lose him, Mr. Owen, that is our great happiness. We shall not lose him, Sara and I, as we had at first feared."

Two tears rolled down her cheeks as she spoke.

"It is because I am so thankful," she said, wiping them away. Her long lace-bordered sleeves had been turned back, and Owen was struck with the old, withered look of her small wrists and hands.

"I could not have borne it to lose him now," she went on, as if explaining. "You may think that existence such as his will be is no blessing, nothing to be desired for him or for me. But he is not suffering, he is even happy as a child is happy, and he knows me. He would be content himself to wait a little, if he could know how much it was to me, how much to have him with me, so that I can devote myself to him, devote myself entirely."

"You have always done that, Madam Carroll," said Owen, touched by her emotion.

"You will come, then—on whatever day the doctor makes up his mind," she said, controlling herself, and returning to her subject.

Here Miss Carroll spoke. "Isn't it better not to make engagements for the present, mamma?" she said, warningly. "You will overtax your strength."

"It is overtaxed at this moment far less than it has been for many a long month," answered Madam Carroll, as it seemed to Owen, strangely. She passed her hand over her forehead, and then, as if putting herself aside in order to consider her companions for a moment, she looked first at Sara, then turned and looked at Owen. "Do not stay any longer now," she said to him, gently, in an advising tone. He obeyed her, and went away.

On the tenth day after this the doctor, whose conclusions, if slowly made, were sure, announced his decision : it tallied exactly with that of Madam Carroll. The Major was in no present danger; his physical health was fairly good ; his condition would not change much, and he might linger on in this state for several years. And then the Far Edgerley people, knowing that no more pain would come to him, and that he was tranquil and even happy, that he recognized his wife, and that she gave to him the most beautiful and tender devotion—then these Far Edgerley people were glad and thankful to have him with them still ; not wholly gone, though lying unseen in his peaceful room, which faced the west, so that the sunset could shine every day upon the quiet sunset of his life. And they thought, some of them, that thanksgiving prayers should be offered for this in the church. And they all prayed for him at home, each family in its own way.

On the afternoon of the day when the doctor had made up his mind, Frederick Owen went to the Farms. Madam Carroll came down to see him ; she took him to the library, now unused, and when they had entered, she closed the door. "Will you sit here beside me?" she said, indicating a sofa opposite the window. Again he was struck by the great—as it seemed to him, the marvellous—change in her. She looked even older than before; her hair was put back in the same plain way; there was the same absence of color, the same tired look in her eyes, the same fine net-work of wrinkles over all her small face; but added to these there was now a settled sadness of expression which he felt would never pass away. He missed, too, all the changing inflections and gestures, the pretty little manner and attitudes, and even the pronunciation, which he had supposed to belong inseparably to her, which he had thought entirely her own. He missed likewise, though unconsciously, the prettiness of the bright little gowns she had always worn; she was dressed now in black, without color or ornament.

She seemed to divine his thoughts. "The Major can no longer see me," she said, quietly; "that is, with any distinctness. It is no longer anything to him—what I wear."

He had taken the seat she had offered; she sat beside him, with her hands folded, her eyes on the opposite wall. "I have a story to tell you," she said. "But I can make no prefaces; I cannot speak of feelings. I hope for your interest, Mr. Owen, even for your sympathy; but if I get them it will be accomplished by a narrative of facts alone, and not by any pathos in the words themselves. I got beyond pathos long ago. My name was Marion More. My father was a missionary in the Southwest—the exact localities I need not give. At sixteen I married. My father died within the year; my mother had died long before. My first child was a son, born when I was seventeen; I called him Julian. Later there came to me a daughter, my little Cecilia. When she was still a baby, and Julian was seven, my husband, in a brawl at a town some miles from our house, killed a man who was well known and liked in the neighborhood; they had both fired, and the other man was the better shot, but upon this occasion his ball happened to miss, and my husband's did not. I was sitting at home, sewing; the baby was in the cradle at my feet, and Julian was playing with his little top on the floor. My husband rode rapidly into the yard on his fast black horse, Tom, sprang down, came into the house, and went into the inner room. He soon came back and went out. He called Julian. The child ran into the yard; then hurried back to get the little overcoat I had made for him. 'Where are you going?' I said. 'To ride with papa,' he answered, and, eager as he was to go, he did not forget to come and kiss me good-by. Then he ran out, and I heard them start;

I heard Tom's hoofs on the hard road farther and
farther away; then all was still. But less than half
an hour afterwards there was noise enough; the garden was full of armed men. The whole country-side
were out after him. They hunted him for three
days. But he knew the woods and swamps better
than they did, and they could not find him. They
knew that he would in time make for the river, and
they kept a watch along shore. He reached it on
the fourth day, at a lonely point; he turned Tom
loose, took a skiff which he knew was there, and
started out with my little boy upon the swollen tide
—for the river was high. They were soon discovered by the watch on shore. Shots were fired at
them. But the skiff was out in the centre of the
stream, which was very wide just there, and the
shots missed. They followed the skiff along shore.
They knew what he did not—that the river narrowed below the bend, and that there were rapids
there. He reached the bend, and saw that he was
lost; the current carried the boat down towards the
narrows; and they began to shoot again; one shot
struck Julian. Then his father took him in his
arms and jumped overboard with him. That, they
knew, was death. They saw the dark bodies whirled
round and round, and amused themselves by shoot-
ing at them once or twice; they saw them sucked

under. Then, farther away, they saw them again
swept along like logs, inert, dead; on and on; two
black dots; out of sight. Then they rode back, that
hunting party; and their wives came and told me,
as mercifully as they could, that my husband and
my little boy were drowned. I could not bury my
dead; on the rapid current of the river they were
already miles away; in that country no one cared
for the dead. They cared but little for the living.
I took my baby and went away; I left that horrible
land. I came eastward. I had no money, or very
little; my husband had taken what—what he needed
for his flight, and there was nothing left. I tried to
teach little day schools for children. I gave music
lessons. I did my best. But I was not strong; my
little girl, too, was very delicate: there was something the matter with her spine. When this life of
ours—hers and mine—had lasted ten years (for I am
much older than you have supposed), I met Major
Carroll. He was so good as to love me; he was so
good as to marry me; he took as his own my poor
little girl, and gave her all the comforts and luxuries
she needed—things I could not give. She died soon
afterwards, in spite of all. But in our new home
she had had happy days, and when the end came
she did not suffer: she went back to God in sleep.
On the 6th of last July I was in the garden here,

gathering some roses; it was below the slope of the
knoll, out of sight from the house. The gate opened,
and a young man came in. He came across to me.
He introduced himself as a stranger in Far Edgerley, who had admired our flowers. He spoke several sentences while I stood looking at him. I was
frightened; I knew not why. At last, recovering
myself, I turned to walk towards the house. Then
it was that he put his hand on my arm, and said:
'Don't you know me, mother? I am Julian, the
little boy you thought dead.' He was thirty-one
years old, and I had lost him before he was eight.
What had startled me was his likeness to his father.
They had escaped, after all. His father had feigned
death; he had let himself be swept along, keeping
hold of the child, who was unconscious. It was a
desperate expedient. But he was desperate. He
was an expert swimmer, and he succeeded, though
barely, with life just fluttering within them. They
lay hid in a canebrake for some days, and then, after
much difficulty, they made their way out of the
country. They went to Mexico. Then they went
to the West India Islands. They lived in Martinique, and they took the name of Dupont. My husband did not try to come back; a reward had been
offered for him before he fled; there was a price on
his head. He knew that I supposed him dead, and

he was quite willing to be dead—to me. He was
tired of me. I was only a burden to him. I was always talking about little things. My son thought that
we were dead—his little sister and I; his father had
told him so. But after his father's death he found
among his papers some memoranda which made him
think that perhaps we were not, that perhaps he
could even find us. He did not try immediately;
it was but a chance, and he was interested in other
things. But later he did try; that is, in his way;
he was never sharp and energetic—as you are. He
found me; but his little sister had gone to heaven.
My son had had only the education of the islands,
and he was, besides, a musician. The temperament
of musicians is peculiar. You will allow me to say
that I think you do not understand it. He wished
to go back to the islands; he had been in the United
States for a year, and he did not like the life or climate. I helped him as much as I could. It was
not much; but he started. Then he had that illness in New York, and came back. It was most
important that he should start again, and soon—before the return of winter. I had nothing to give
him, and so I went to my daughter—I mean my step-
daughter, Sara. She has, you know, a small income of
her own, left her by her uncle. You are asking yourself why I did not go to the Major; why there should
14

have been any secret about it from the first. It was because I had not told him at the time of our marriage, or at any time, that I had ever had a son. He thought when he married me that Cecilia was my only child; he thought me twenty-three, when I was in reality over thirty-five. It would have been a great shock and pain to him to know that I had deceived him—a shock which, in his state of health at that time, he could not have borne. When Sara knew, she helped me; she helped me nobly. But the time for the semi-annual payment of her income was not until the 12th of October, and by the terms of her uncle's will she could not anticipate it; we were therefore obliged to wait. Before the 12th of October my son was taken ill, as I had feared. And the rest—you know. The time when I could tell you this has now come. It has come because nothing can again disturb the Major's peace. He is near us in touch, and close to our love, but earth's sorrows and pains can trouble him no more. I can therefore tell you, and I do it for two reasons. One is that it will explain to you the course we took; it will explain to you what Sara said that afternoon, for I think that it has grieved you—what Sara said. It was an expedient that she thought of to divert your attention, to stop further action on your part. We knew — from your having tried to see the Major,

and see him alone—that you had learned something; how much, we could not tell. And when
you came again the next day, and spoke as you did,
first to me, and then to her, and I was frightened
and lost my courage, fearing lest you should speak
to others also; then Sara took the only expedient
she could think of to silence you, to stop you effectually, and thus secure her father's peace. But
it was only an expedient, Mr. Owen. It was never
true." She paused for the first time in the utterance of her brief sentences, turned her head, and
looked at him with her faded, tired eyes.

Owen's own eyes were wet. "Even before that,"
he said, "and I do not deny how important it is
to me—more important than anything else in the
world—even before that, Madam Carroll, I beg you
to say that you forgive me, that you forgive what I
did and said. I did not know—how could I?—and
I was greatly troubled."

"I think I can say that I have forgiven you," answered Madam Carroll. "I did not at first; I did
not for a long time. It is all over now; and of
course you did not know. But you never understood my son—you could not; and therefore—if you
will be so good—I should prefer that you should not
speak to me of him again; it is much the easiest
way for us both." She turned her eyes back to the

wall. "About Sara," she continued, without pause, "it was a pity. It has been a long time for you to wait—with that—that mistaken belief on your mind. But, while the Major was still with us in his consciousness and his memory, I could not tell to you, a stranger, what I was not able to tell him."

"You were afraid to trust me!" said Owen, a pained expression coming into his face.

"Yes," answered Madam Carroll, simply.

"You did not know then that I felt as far as possible from being a stranger? That I wished—that I have tried—"

"That is later; I was coming to that. Yes—since I have known that you cared so much for her (though I knew it long ago!)—since you have spoken, rather, I have felt that I wished to tell you, that I would gladly tell you, as soon as I could. The time has come, and it came earlier than I expected, though I knew it could not be long delayed. I have taken the earliest hour."

"Then she—then Miss Carroll told you that I— that I had spoken?" said Owen.

"She told me because I asked her, pressed her. I knew that you had been here—a week ago, wasn't it?—I had caught a glimpse of your face as you left the house. And so I asked her. She is very reticent, very proud; she would never have told me, in spite of my asking, if her wish to show me that I had been mistaken in something I had said to her long before had not been stronger even than her reserve."

"What was it that you were mistaken in ?" said Owen, quickly.

"I was not mistaken. But she wished to prove to me that I was. I had told her in October that she cared for you, and that she had made the greatest sacrifice a woman could make in voluntarily lowering herself in your eyes by allowing you to suppose—to suppose what you did."

"You were mistaken, after all, Madam Carroll," said Owen, sadly. "She cares nothing for me."

" Men are dull," answered the mistress of the Farms, wearily. "They have to have everything explained to them. Don't you see that it was inevitable that she should refuse you ? As things stood—as you let them stand—she could not stoop to any other course. She knew that you believed that she had cared for— for Louis Dupont" (Madam Carroll's face had here a strange, set sternness, but her soft voice went on unchanged), "and she knew your opinion of him. She knew, moreover, that you believed it clandestine, that she had not dared to tell her father. For you to come, then, at this late day, believing all this, and tell her that you loved her—that seemed to her an

insult. Your tone was, I presume (if not your words),
that you loved her in spite of all."

"Yes," Owen answered. "For that was my feeling. I did love her in spite of all. I had fought
against it. I had thought — I don't know what.
But it was over; whatever it had been it was ended
forever, and my love had conquered. I knew *that*
very well!"

"And you told her so, I suppose—'I love you in
spite of all'—when you should have said 'I love
you; and it never existed.'"

"But had she not told me with her own lips that
it did exist, that she was engaged to him?"

"You should not have believed her own lips; you
should have risen above that. You should have told
her to her face that you did not believe, and never
would believe, anything that was, or even seemed to
be, against her. I see you know very little about
women. You will have to learn. I am taking all
this pains for you because I want her to be happy.
Her nature is a very noble one, in spite of an over-
weight of pride. She could not explain to you, even
at that time, without betraying me, and that she
would never do. But I doubt whether she would
have explained in any case; it would have been doing too much for you."

"All she did was done for her father," said Owen;

"and it was the same with you, Madam Carroll.
Seldom has man been so loved. My place with her
will be but a second one."

"That should content you."

"Ah, you do *not* like me, though you try to help
me," cried the young man. "But give me time,
Madam Carroll; give me time."

"To make me like you? Take as much as you
please. But do not take it with Sara."

"I shall take five minutes," Owen answered. Then
he lifted her hand to his lips. "Forgive me for
thinking of my own happiness," he said, with the
gentlest respect."

"I like you to think of it; it gives me pleasure.
And now I must come to my second reason for telling you. You remember I said that there were two.
This is something which even Sara does not know—
I would not give her any of that burden; she could
not help me, and she had enough to bear. She could
not help me; but now you can. It is something I
want you to do for me. It could not be done before, it could not be done until the Major became as
he is at present. No one now living knows; still,
as you are to be one of us, I should like to have you
do it for me."

And then she told him.

CHAPTER IX.

On Easter Sunday morning Far Edgerley people woke to find their village robed in blossoms; in one night the fruit trees had burst into bloom, so that all the knolls and Edgerley Street itself stood in bridal array, and walking to church was like taking part in a beautiful procession.

Nearly a month had passed since the Major's attack; but all his old friends in the congregation of St. John's missed him more than ever on this Easter morning. Sara and Scar were in the Carroll pew at the head of the aisle; but it looked very empty, nevertheless. During this month there had not been much change in the Major, save that for two weeks after the doctor's decision he had not been so well; restlessness had troubled him. But for the preceding few days he had been much better, and every one was cheered by this; every one was interested in hearing that he had talked quite at length with his wife on simple local subjects, that he enjoyed little things, and thought about them. He lived en-

tirely in the present, the present of the passing moment; everything in the past he had forgotten, and
he speedily forgot the moment itself as soon as it
was gone. What his wife said to him he understood,
and he always knew when she was near, though his
blind eyes could not see her; he felt for a fold of
her dress or the ruffle of her sleeve, and held it; the
sense of touch had taken the place of the vanished
sight. He listened for Scar's voice too, and seemed
to like to have him in the room, to hold the child's
hand in his. In the same way he always smiled and
was pleased when Sara spoke to him.

When the morning service was over, every one
waited to ask how the Major was on this lovely
Easter Sunday. Lately they had come to like his
daughter far better than they had liked her at first;
they said she talked more, that she was not so cold.
Certainly there was nothing cold in her face, but a
beautiful sweetness, as she rose from her knees and,
taking Scar's hand, turned to go down the aisle. She
answered their questions on the steps and in the
church-yard. For on Easter morning Far Edgerley
people always brought many flowers to church;
then, after service, they took them out and laid them
upon all the graves, so that, as Scar once said, "they
could have their Easter Sunday too." Every mound
had its blossoms to-day, and there were many upon

the grave of the young stranger, Louis Dupont; this was because there was no one, they said, to remember him. So they all remembered him.

A little before sunset Frederick Owen, having officiated at the Easter service of the Sunday-school and at one of his mission stations, was on his way to Carroll Farms. As he came up Carroll Lane and crossed the little bridge over the brook, he saw that there was more bloom here than anywhere else in all the blooming town. For the whole orchard was out behind the house, and all the flowering almonds in front of it; the old stone walls rose close pressed in blossoms. Sara opened the door before he had time to knock. "I was watching for you," she said. "Judith Inches and Caleb have gone up the mountain to see their mother, as they always do on Easter afternoon, and they have taken Scar."

Owen paused in the hall to greet her; he was very proud of this proud, reserved girl whose love he had won.

"Do not wait, Frederick. Mamma has such a pleadingly sorrowful look to-day that I want to have it over."

"Only a moment," said Owen. He was standing with his arm round her, holding her close. "Do you remember that afternoon when I spoke to you of your mother, of the sisterly kindness she had

shown to that poor woman who had lost her crippled boy? And do you remember that you said
that no one save those who were in the house with
her all the time could comprehend the one hundredth
part of her tenderness, her constant thought for others? Your answer put me in a glow of pleasure, I
did not then comprehend why. I asked myself as
I walked home if I cared so much to hear Madam
Carroll praised. I know now what I cared for—it
was because *you* had said it. For I had been afraid,
unconsciously to myself, perhaps, that you did not
fully appreciate her, appreciate her as she seemed to
me."

"And I had not until then. I shall always reproach myself—"

"You need not; you have made up for it a hun-
dredfold," answered Owen. Then, coming back to
himself, with love's unfailing egotism—"I wonder if
you realize all the suffering I went through?" he
continued. "You made me wait in my pain so long,
so long!"

"We suffer more than you do, always," answered,
after a moment, the woman he held in his arms.
And then into her beautiful eyes, raised to meet his,
there came such a world of feeling, some of it beyond his ken, that touched, stirred, feeling himself
unworthy, yet exultant in his happiness, the man

who loved her rested his lips on hers without at-
tempting further reply.

A moment later he went up the stairs, and Sara
turned the key of the front door. The Major, his
wife and daughter, and the clergyman were now
alone in the flower - encircled house. All its windows were open, and the flowers fairly seemed to be
coming in, so near were they to the casements; outside the Major's windows two great apple - trees, a
mass of bloom, stretched out their long, flowering
arms until they touched the sills.

The sun, now low down, was sinking towards Lonely mountain; he sent horizontal rays full into the
mass of apple-blossoms, but could not penetrate them
save as a faintly pink radiance, which fell upon the
figure of Madam Carroll as she stood beside the bed.
She wore one of her white dresses, but her face looked
worn and old as the radiance brought out all its lines,
and showed the many silver threads in her faded
hair. The Major was sitting up in bed; he had on a
new dressing-gown, and was propped with cushions.

"Has the clergyman come?" he said. He spoke
indistinctly, but his wife could always understand
him.

"Yes, he is here, Scarborough," she answered,
bending over him.

"He is welcome. Let him be seated," said the

Major, in his old ceremonial manner. Then he felt
for his wife's arm, and pulled her sleeve. "Am I
dressed?" he asked, anxiously. "Did you see to it?
Is my hair smooth?" He supposed himself to be
speaking in a whisper.

"Yes, Major, you have on your new dressing-
gown, and it is of a beautiful color, and your hair
is quite smooth."

"I don't feel sure about the hair," said the Major,
still, as he supposed, confidentially. "I don't remember that I brushed it."

Madam Carroll took a brush from the table and
gently smoothed the thin white locks.

"That is better," he murmured. "And my clean
white silk handkerchief?"

"It is by your side, close to your hand."

He thought for a moment. "I ought to have a
flower for my button-hole, oughtn't I?" he added,
looking about the room with his darkened eyes as
if to find one.

Sara went to the window and broke off a spray
of apple-blossoms from the tree outside. His wife
gave it to him, and he tried to put it into the button-
hole of his dressing-gown; she did it for him, and
then he was content. "I am ready now," he said,
folding his hands.

Frederick Owen came forward; he wore his white

robes of office. "Dearly beloved, we are gathered together here in the sight of God to join together this man and this woman in holy matrimony," he read, standing close to the Major, so that he could hear.

The Major listened with serenity; and of his own accord, when the time came, he answered, "I will."

When the longer answer was reached, Owen repeated it first, then Madam Carroll repeated it to the Major, as he could hear her voice more easily. "I, Scarborough, take thee, Marion, to my wedded wife, to have and to hold from this day forward, for better for worse, for richer for poorer, in sickness and in health, to love and to cherish, till death us do part, according to God's holy ordinance; and thereto I plight thee my troth," said the Major, in his indistinct tones, following her word by word, and holding the hand she had placed in his.

Then the wife drew off her own wedding-ring, and guided his feeble fingers to put it back in its place again. "With this ring I thee wed," said the Major, repeating after her in a voice that was growing tired.

"Let us pray," said Owen. They knelt, and the Major bowed his head, and put his hand over his eyes. "Our Father, who art in heaven," prayed Owen, "hallowed be thy name."

As he came to the benediction, the sun's last rays, sent from the golden line of Lonely Mountain, shot triumphantly under the apple-blossoms and entered the room; they shone on Madam Carroll's kneeling figure, and lighted up the old Major's silver hair— "that in the world to come, ye may have life everlasting. Amen."

There was a silence. Then the Major took down his hand and tried to look from one to the other as they stood round his bed. His wife kissed him. And then Sara, her eyes full of tears, came and kissed him also.

"Where is the clergyman?" said the Major to his wife, again supposing himself to be speaking apart. "I ought to shake hands with him, you know."

Owen came forward, and the Major bowed and put out his hand. Then he seemed to be forgetting all that had occurred. "I am very tired, Marion," he said, not complainingly, but as if surprised. "I don't know what is the reason, but I am very tired." They took out the cushions, and he put his head down upon the pillow. In a few minutes he was asleep.

At late twilight Scar came back in the wagon with Judith Inches and Caleb. His mother was waiting for him on the piazza; she took him in her arms and kissed him several times. "Why, mamma, you are crying!" said the boy, surprised. "Are you sorry about anything, mamma?"

"Yes, Scar. But it is over now. Come up-stairs."

The Major was awake; he looked very tranquil. Sara was sitting beside him. Scar went up to the bedside. "It is Scar," said Madam Carroll. "Don't you remember him, Major? Little Scar?"

"Certainly," said the Major. "Of course I remember him; a little child."

She took his hand and put it on the boy's head. The Major stroked the fair hair gently. "Little Scar," he murmured softly to himself. "Yes, certainly I remember; little Scar."

THE END.

A Novel.

By CONSTANCE FENIMORE WOOLSON.

ILLUSTRATED BY REINHART.

16mo, Cloth, $1.25.

EXTRACTS FROM NOTICES OF "ANNE."

It proves the author's right to stand without question at the head of American women novelists.—*N. Y. Tribune.*

The appearance of "Anne" may be regarded as a fact worth special notice, for Miss Woolson adds to her observation of scenes and localities an unusual insight into the human heart. Sometimes one is ready to say that a fragment, and not an inferior fragment, of the mantle of George Eliot is resting on her capable shoulders. —*Century,* N. Y.

The scenery is fine, the characterization excellent, and the purpose true. * * * It has fine touches. * * * It has admirable sketches from nature. * * * The book has humor, also, and plenty of it. * * * Anne is full of power, and will not soon be forgotten.—*Literary World,* Boston.

A very vigorous story. * * * Anne is very well drawn, and is an attractive study.—*Zion's Herald,* Boston.

A rich contribution to American fiction.—*Christian Intelligencer,* N.Y.

It is one of the most remarkable combinations of feminine delicacy and acuteness with masculine strength and breadth furnished by a lady novelist since "Uncle Tom's Cabin" was given to the public. * * * Of the heroine we can only say she is wholly admirable—a perfect woman. The plot is unique, of increasing interest, presenting many varied and novel scenes, and alternating artistically between the lighter and deeper emotions. The author exerts her dramatic powers to the utmost toward the close, and the result is something rarely paralleled in modern fiction.—*Pittsburgh Christian Advocate.*

Its wealth of plot, its rare bits of humor, its well-marked characterization, and its many fine pieces of description of natural scenery.— *San Francisco Chronicle.*

Its characters are marvels. They are not portraits nor statues, but living persons among and of us. Anne is a type, first of girlhood, then womanhood, of wondrous beauty—an imperishable flower of that wild, almost uncivilized, rugged region whence alone she could have sprung.—*Cleveland Leader.*

A strong, fresh, vigorous story, American in scene, people, and tone. * * * Few novels contain more striking incidents.—*Louisville Courier-Journal.*

One of the cleverest of recent American novels.—*N. Y. World.*

The publication of a book like Miss Woolson's "Anne" is really a literary event. * * * The plot is carefully studied, and is worked out with an honest patience and a conscientious faithfulness in details which merit the name of genius.—*Dial,* Chicago.

Clearly a work of genius.—*Boston Traveller.*

A book which has excited more interest and expectation during its appearance in serial form than any American novel published for years. * * * "Anne" is a work of real power; its characters are painted with a master hand; its literary style calls for the warmest praise; and the story has pre-eminently that sympathetic quality which is the chief charm of what may be called the novel of domestic life.—*Saturday Evening Gazette,* Boston.

"Anne" has produced a very marked impression—more so, indeed, than any other recent work of fiction. * * * It certainly is a delightful and refreshing novel.—*Albany Evening Journal.*

A delightful novel of American life.—*Portland Transcript.*

A charming domestic story, interesting in plot and incident, and fresh in the telling.—*St. Louis Republican.*

It is one of the strongest and most perfectly finished American novels ever written.—*New England Farmer,* Boston.

To take up this volume is to hold it until every page has been read. The interest is kept up without intermission from beginning to end, for new complications and developments arise so constantly that the reader is kept on the *qui vive.*—*Pittsburgh Telegraph.*

PUBLISHED BY HARPER & BROTHERS, NEW YORK.

☞ *Sent by mail, postage prepaid, to any part of the United States, on receipt of the price.*

SOME POPULAR NOVELS

Published by HARPER & BROTHERS, New York.

The Novels in this list which are not otherwise designated are in Octavo, pamphlet form, and may be obtained in half-binding [leather backs and pasteboard sides], suitable for Public and Circulating Libraries, at 25 cents, net, per volume, in addition to the price of the respective works as stated below. The Duodecimo Novels are bound in Cloth, unless otherwise specified.

For a FULL LIST OF NOVELS published by HARPER & BROTHERS, see HARPER'S NEW AND REVISED CATALOGUE, which will be sent by mail, postage prepaid, to any address in the United States, on receipt of nine cents.

PRICE

CRAIK'S (Miss G. M.) Sylvia's Choice..............................$ 30
　Two Women..4to, Paper 15
COLLINS'S Antonina.. 40
　Armadale. Illustrated.. 60
　Man and Wife. Illustrated... 60
　　　　　　　　　　　　　　　　　　　　4to, Paper 15
　My Lady's Money....................................32mo, Paper 25
　No Name. Illustrated... 60
　Percy and the Prophet...............................32mo, Paper 20
　Poor Miss Finch. Illustrated...................................... 60
　The Law and the Lady. Illustrated............................... 50
　The Moonstone. Illustrated....................................... 60
　The New Magdalen.. 30
　The Two Destinies. Illustrated................................... 35
　The Woman in White. Illustrated................................ 60
COLLINS'S Illustrated Library Edition.............12mo, per vol. 1 25
　After Dark, and Other Stories.—Antonina.—Armadale.—
　　Basil. — Hide-and-Seek. — Man and Wife. — My Miscel-
　　lanies.—No Name.—Poor Miss Finch.—The Dead Secret.
　　—The Law and the Lady.—The Moonstone.—The New
　　Magdalen.—The Queen of Hearts.—The Two Destinies.
　　—The Woman in White.

DICKENS'S NOVELS. Illustrated.

A Tale of Two Cities...	50		Nicholas Nickleby		1 00
	Cloth	1 00		Cloth	1 50
Barnaby Rudge	1 00		Oliver Twist		50
	Cloth	1 50		Cloth	1 00
Bleak House	1 00		Our Mutual Friend		1 00
	Cloth	1 50		Cloth	1 50
Christmas Stories	1 00		Pickwick Papers		1 00
	Cloth	1 50		Cloth	1 50
David Copperfield	1 00			4to, Paper	20
	Cloth	1 50	Pictures from Italy, Sketch-		
Dombey and Son	1 00		es by Boz, and American		
	Cloth	1 50	Notes		1 00
Great Expectations	1 00			Cloth	1 50
	Cloth	1 50	The Old Curiosity Shop		75
Little Dorrit	1 00			Cloth	1 25
	Cloth	1 50	The Uncommercial Traveller,		
Martin Chuzzlewit	1 00		Hard Times, and Edwin		
	Cloth	1 50	Drood		1 00
				Cloth	1 50

Harper's Household Dickens, 16 vols., Cloth, in box, $22 00.
　The same in 8 vols., Cloth, $20 00 ; Imitation Half Mo-
　rocco, $22 00 ; Half Calf, $40 00.
DE MILLE'S Cord and Creese. Illustrated......................... 60
　The American Baron. Illustrated................................ 50
　The Cryptogram. Illustrated..................................... 75

PRICE

DE MILLE'S The Dodge Club. Illustrated.......................$ 60

                                                 Cloth 1 10

   The Living Link. Illustrated....................................... 60

                                                 Cloth 1 10

DISRAELI'S (Earl of Beaconsfield) Endymion ....4to, Paper 15

   The Young Duke..12mo 1 50

                                         4to, Paper 15

ELIOT'S (George) Novels:

   Adam Bede. Illustrated..................................12mo 1 25

   Amos Barton...32mo, Paper 20

   Brother Jacob.—The Lifted Veil...............32mo, Paper 20

   Daniel Deronda.. 50

                                    2 vols., 12mo 2 50

   Felix Holt, the Radical...................................... 50

                               Illustrated. 12mo 1 25

   Janet's Repentance..................................32mo, Paper 20

   Middlemarch 75

                                          Cloth 1 25

                                  2 vols., 12mo 2 50

   Mr. Gilfil's Love Story...........................32mo, Paper 20

   Romola. Illustrated... 50

                                          12mo 1 25

   Scenes of Clerical Life.. 50

   Scenes of Clerical Life and Silas Marner. 1 vol. Ill'd. 12mo 1 25

   Silas Marner...12mo 75

   The Mill on the Floss.. 50

                                  Illustrated. 12mo 1 25

GASKELL'S (Mrs.) A Dark Night's Work....................... 25

   Cousin Phillis... 20

   Cranford...16mo 1 25

   Mary Barton 40

   Moorland Cottage...18mo 75

   My Lady Ludlow.. 20

   North and South... 40

   Right at Last, &c..12mo 1 50

   Sylvia's Lovers.. 40

   Wives and Daughters. Illustrated......................... 60

GOLDSMITH'S Vicar of Wakefield.....................18mo, Cloth 50

                                 32mo, Paper 25

HAY'S (M. C.) A Dark Inheritance....................32mo, Paper 15

   A Shadow on the Threshold.......................32mo, Paper 20

   Among the Ruins, and Other Stories.........4to, Paper 15

   At the Seaside, and Other Stories..............4to, Paper 15

   Back to the Old Home.............................32mo, Paper 20

   Bid Me Discourse.................................4to, Paper 10

   Dorothy's Venture.................................4to, Paper 15

   For Her Dear Sake...............................4to, Paper 15

   Hidden Perils... 25

PRICE

HAY'S (M. C.) Into the Shade, and Other Stories...4to, Paper $ .15
    Lady Carmichael's Will.............................32mo, Paper   15
    Missing..32mo, Paper   20
    My First Offer, and Other Stories....................4to, Paper   15
    Nora's Love Test.....................................   25
    Old Myddelton's Money................................   25
    Reaping the Whirlwind...........................32mo, Paper   20
    The Arundel Motto...................................   25
    The Sorrow of a Secret..........................32mo, Paper   15
    The Squire's Legacy.................................   25
    Under Life's Key, and Other Stories.................4to, Paper   15
    Victor and Vanquished...............................   25
HELEN Troy...16mo, Cloth 1 00
HUGO'S Ninety-Three. Illustrated....................   25
                                12mo 1 75
    The Toilers of the Sea..............................   50
                             Illustrated. Cloth 1 50
JAMES'S (Henry, Jun.) Daisy Miller................32mo, Paper   20
    An International Episode.........................32mo, Paper   20
    Diary of a Man of Fifty, and A Bundle of Letters............
                                  32mo, Paper   25
    *The four above-mentioned works in one volume.*4to, Paper   25
    Washington Square. Illustrated...................16mo, Cloth 1 25
LAWRENCE'S Anteros..................................   40
    Brakespeare...   40
    Breaking a Butterfly................................   35
    Guy Livingstone.................................12mo 1 50
                              4to, Paper   10
    Hagarene...   35
    Maurice Dering.....................................   25
    Sans Merci...   35
    Sword and Gown.....................................   20
LEVER'S A Day's Ride................................   40
    Barrington...   40
    Gerald Fitzgerald..................................   40
    Lord Kilgobbin. Illustrated........................   50
    Luttrell of Arran..................................   60
    Maurice Tiernay....................................   50
    One of Them..   50
    Roland Cashel. Illustrated.........................   75
    Sir Brook Fosbrooke................................   50
    Sir Jasper Carew...................................   50
    That Boy of Norcott's. Illustrated.................   25
    The Bramleighs of Bishop's Folly...................   50
    The Daltons..   75
    The Dodd Family Abroad.............................   60
    The Fortunes of Glencore...........................   50
    The Martins of Cro' Martin.........................   60

PRICE

PAYN'S (James) Cecil's Tryst...$ 30
    For Cash Only...4to, Paper 20
    Found Dead... 25
    From Exile...4to, Paper 15
    Gwendoline's Harvest... 25
    Halves... 30
    High Spirits...4to, Paper 15
    Kit. Illustrated..4to, Paper 20
    Less Black than We're Painted... 35
    Murphy's Master.. 20
    One of the Family.. 25
    The Best of Husbands... 25
    Under One Roof...4to, Paper 15
    Walter's Word.. 50
    What He Cost Her... 40
    Won—Not Wooed.. 35

READE'S Novels: Household Edition. Ill'd......12mo, per vol. 1 00

A Simpleton and the Wandering Heir.	It is Never Too Late to Mend.
	Love me Little, Love me Long.
A Terrible Temptation.	Peg Woffington, Christie Johnstone, &c.
A Woman-Hater.	
Foul Play.	Put Yourself in His Place.
Griffith Gaunt.	The Cloister and the Hearth.
Hard Cash.	White Lies.

READE'S (Charles) A Hero and a Martyr............................. 15
    A Simpleton.. 35
    A Terrible Temptation. Illustrated.. 40
    A Woman-Hater. Illustrated.. 60
    Foul Play.. 35
    Griffith Gaunt. Illustrated... 40
    Hard Cash. Illustrated.. 50
    It is Never Too Late to Mend.. 50
    Love Me Little, Love Me Long.. 35
    Multum in Parvo...4to, Paper 15
    Peg Woffington, &c.. 50
    Put Yourself in His Place. Illustrated.................................... 50
    The Cloister and the Hearth... 50
    The Jilt...32mo, Paper 20
    The Wandering Heir. Illustrated... 25
    White Lies... 40

RICE & BESANT'S All Sorts and Conditions of Men...4to, Paper 20
    By Celia's Arbor. Illustrated.............................8vo, Paper 50
    Shepherds All and Maidens Fair...........................32mo, Paper 25
    "So they were Married!" Illustrated.......................4to, Paper 20
    Sweet Nelly, My Heart's Delight..........................4to, Paper 10
    The Captains' Room..4to, Paper 10
    The Chaplain of the Fleet................................4to, Paper 20

PRICE

TROLLOPE'S (Anthony) The Eustace Diamonds.   Illustrated..$ 80
The Fixed Period...4to, Paper   15
The Golden Lion of Granpere.   Illustrated....................   40
The Lady of Launay.................................32mo, Paper   20
The Last Chronicle of Barset.   Illustrated....................   90
The Prime Minister..   60
The Small House at Allington.   Illustrated.............   75
The Three Clerks...12mo 1 50
The Vicar of Bullhampton.   Illustrated......................   80
The Warden, and Barchester Towers.   In one volume.......   60
The Way We Live Now.   Illustrated..........................   90
Thompson Hall.   Illustrated......................32mo, Paper   20
Why Frau Frohman Raised her Prices, &c.........4to, Paper   10
TROLLOPE'S (T. A.) Lindisfarn Chase..........................   60
A Siren..   40
Durnton Abbey..........   40
Diamond Cut Diamond 12mo 1 25
WALLACE'S (Lew) Ben-Hur.............................16mo, Cloth 1 50
WAVERLEY NOVELS:
   THISTLE EDITION: 48 Vols., Green Cloth, with 2000
   Illustrations, $1 00 per vol.; Half Morocco, Gilt Tops,
   $1 50 per vol.; Half Morocco, Extra, $2 25 per vol.
   HOLYROOD EDITION: 48 Vols., Brown Cloth, with 2000
   Illustrations, 75 cents per vol.; Half Morocco, Gilt Tops,
   $1 50 per vol.; Half Morocco, Extra, $2 25 per vol.
   POPULAR EDITION: 24 Vols. (two vols. in one), Green
   Cloth, with 2000 Illustrations, $1 25 per vol.; Half Moroc-
   co, $2 25 per vol. ; Half Morocco, Extra, $3 00 per vol.
   Waverley; Guy Mannering; The Antiquary; Rob Roy;
   Old Mortality; The Heart of Mid-Lothian; A Legend of
   Montrose; The Bride of Lammermoor; The Black Dwarf;
   Ivanhoe; The Monastery; The Abbot; Kenilworth; The
   Pirate; The Fortunes of Nigel; Peveril of the Peak;
   Quentin Durward; St. Ronan's Well; Redgauntlet; The
   Betrothed; The Talisman; Woodstock; Chronicles of the
   Canongate, The Highland Widow, &c.; The Fair Maid of
   Perth; Anne of Geierstein; Count Robert of Paris; Cas-
   tle Dangerous; The Surgeon's Daughter; Glossary.
WOOLSON'S (C. F.) Anne.   Illustrated................16mo, Cloth 1 25
For the Major.   Illustrated.......................16mo, Cloth
YATES'S (Edmund) Black Sheep................................   40
Kissing the Rod   40
Land at Last...   40
Wrecked in Port...   35
Dr. Wainwright's Patient................................   30

☞ HARPER & BROTHERS *will send any of the above works by mail, postage prepaid, to any part of the United States, on receipt of the price.*